ONE OF THEM
GIRLS

CALA RILEY

Cover Photo by: Y'all That Graphic
Formatting by: Books and Moods
Editing done by: My Brothers Editor

All women are crazy.

Love
Cala

+ Riley

CHAPTER ONE

Xavier

"Hey, man," Jack calls out to someone as we walk through the house party.

Part of me is surprised that he knows so many people already. We've only been here a week.

"Hey Jack, who's this guy?" some random guy asks.

"My roommate, Xavier. He's new to Texas."

I half-wave while looking around, taking in the scene before me. I don't know why I was thinking a house party here with college kids would be any different. It's just like any other house party. Well, except the ones back at Brighton. That has more to do with the wealth being thrown around than the actual party itself.

I follow Jack through the house and into the kitchen where two kegs are on ice and a counter full of liquor.

"Here's a beer." Jack shoves a cup in my hand. "Try to enjoy yourself."

I take the beer, making my way to the edge of the room. Finding an open spot, I lean against the wall.

It's your run-of-the-mill frat house. Small rooms with furniture pushed against walls to make more room. I let my eyes wander over the dance floor. Mostly women gyrating against one another, casting quick glances to the guys standing around watching. A couple of the guys have joined in on the fun, their hands sliding all over their partners' bodies.

One couple breaks off, heading upstairs.

I shake my head and take a sip of the warm beer. Gross. I set it down on the floor next to me and continue to people watch.

I suppose this is better than staring at my ceiling.

A couple of the girls try to catch my eye, but I'm quick to avoid them. I don't need any drama, and these girls have drama written all over them.

My phone buzzes in my pocket. Taking it out, I see a text from Tinsley. I had texted her earlier, letting her know I was going out.

> **Tinsley:** Yay! I'm so glad you went out. Have fun and tell me all about it tomorrow. Finley says don't forget to wrap it before you tap it.

I chuckle. Finley would say that. I'm about to respond when a body runs into mine.

I look up from my phone to tell the person to fuck off, but freeze.

Her eyes trap me in their gaze. She's gorgeous. Her head comes up to my shoulders, so she has to lean her head back to look at me.

Her long, blonde hair is curled, falling down her back, highlighting her bright blue-green eyes looking up at me expectantly.

What does she want?

I don't know, but I sure as fuck might be willing to give it to her.

My heart beats heavy in my chest. This is the first time since *her* I've felt anything for a woman.

Fuck.

"Hey, babe. There you are." Her hands settle on my chest.

Absentmindedly, my hands fall to her hips. I stay silent, questioning what she's doing.

"This is the guy you're meeting up with?"

I glance over her shoulder as I see a guy Jack introduced me to earlier.

She leans up, kissing the side of my mouth and damn it if I don't want to turn into her, but I stay still.

"Yep. This is the new guy I've been dating. So as you can see, you can run along."

Suspicion lines his eyes, so I pull her closer and whisper in her ear, "Giggle like I'm telling you something dirty. He's not buying your act."

On cue, she giggles, pressing her body even closer to mine. Then she leans up and whispers in my ear, "My name's Cassandra."

"Xavier," I respond.

And just like that, we are having our own private conversation in whispers. I glance once more over her shoulder to see the guy stomp off.

"Your ex just stomped off. I think you're in the clear."

She leans back, rolling her eyes. "He's not my ex. It's a long story. I should go home though. I knew it was a bad idea to show up here."

She pulls out of my grip.

"Let me walk you out," I tell her.

"No, you don't need to do that. Really." I see a faint blush cover her cheeks.

"What kind of guy would I be if I didn't even walk my girl out?" I quirk an eyebrow.

She smiles. "I guess you're right."

I wrap my arm around her shoulder as I escort her to the door. I give a two-finger wave to Jack as we move through the party. He gives me a confused look, but waves back.

I watch as she gives her own across the room goodbye to a girl, but instead of confusion, she gets a thumbs up.

Once outside and a few houses down, Cassandra shrugs out of my embrace. I give her a little distance.

"This is weird," she says, breaking the silence. "I shouldn't be going anywhere with you really, let alone let you know where I live. I can hear my brother cursing me for my idiocy."

I chuckle. "You're right. You shouldn't be out walking with a stranger and leading him back to your place. It's dangerous. You know what else is dangerous? Rescuing a damsel in distress only to find out she's luring me to her den. Maybe I should be the one worried."

She lets out a full-body laugh, shaking from the intensity. Making me laugh with her.

"That's a good one." She reaches out to pat my arm.

"You can never be too careful. I mean, you have a crazy ex that I had to save you from. Who's to say he isn't following us, waiting to beat my ass then rob me?"

This time she lets out a small laugh, looking a little uncomfortable. "He's not my ex," she repeats. "He's my brother's best friend. It's a really long and complicated story I'd prefer not to get into."

Baggage.

She has a lot of emotional baggage. I get that. I don't really want to get into my shit either, so I change the subject.

"Ah. I see. Little sister has guards. Guess I should be more careful around you. They could pop out from anywhere." I jump as if I saw something in the shadows, pushing her in front of me as a shield.

She lets out another genuine laugh. "How chivalrous. Push me in the way."

I hold up my hands in surrender. "Hey. They're your bodyguards. They're unlikely to hurt you. I'm trying to preserve this pretty face."

As she laughs, I watch as the last bit of sadness leaves her body.

"No bodyguards. Just trying to get him to realize I'm a big girl. I can take care of myself. He's having a problem seeing that."

"Ah, that I understand," I reply, thinking of Tinsley and her brothers.

My phone buzzes in my pocket, but I make no move to look at it.

"You can answer it, you know. It might be important."

I pull out my phone and see a video message from Tinsley.

Speak of the devil.

I swipe the screen, starting the video.

"It's so beautiful here. You would love it. Wish you were here."

"But kinda glad you're not."

"Finley! Love you, X! Have fun!"

The video stops and I laugh, shoving my phone back into my pocket.

"Girlfriend?" Cassandra asks, side-eyeing me as we walk.

"Nah, not my girlfriend. It was my best friend, Tinsley, and her man Finley." I shrug.

"Anything ever happen between you two?" she asks, looking forward.

"Nah, not really. Her heart always belonged to Fin, and it was obvious to everyone but him."

"So a guy can really be friends with a girl without falling in love with her, huh?"

"I guess so."

We fall into silence as we walk side-by-side. I think about the girl I lost.

Can you really lose someone when they were never yours to begin with?

"So, tell me something about yourself Cassandra?" I say, breaking the silence.

"What do you want to know?"

"How old are you? Have you figured out a major yet? The typical stuff."

"Well, I'm eighteen. I'm from a small town nearby and I'm not completely set on a major yet. You?"

"Eighteen, from New York but moved from the Chicago area, and I'm majoring in education."

"Long way from home," she teases, making me laugh.

"Yeah, it's a little different here than what I'm used to." I rub my jaw.

"Well." Cassandra slows her pace. "This is me." She points to the building next to me.

"Then it looks like I got you home safe."

"You did, such a gentleman." She smiles. "Maybe I'll see you around sometime," she says, walking backward toward her building.

"You probably will." I shove my hands into my pockets and nod at the door. "I'll walk away once you're inside."

"Nice meeting you, Xavier," she calls over her shoulder, stepping inside the building.

"Nice meeting you too, Cassandra," I murmur to myself.

As I walk home, I think about the pretty blonde girl and not once do I think about the one who usually consumes my thoughts.

Cassi

"WHERE DID YOU disappear off to last night?" Rebecca, my roommate, asks as soon as I come in from my classes.

"Jared was being an asshole, so I left," I tell her.

"From what I hear, you have a new boyfriend you left with," she teases.

"More like some poor sap that got sucked into my drama with Jared."

"Tell me everything. Jared was pissed when you left. Then Samantha said she saw you leave with that yummy guy from out east."

I roll my eyes. Of course, Samantha knows about Xavier. She's always on the hunt for her next great romance. The hotter, the better, and Xavier's the embodiment of hot as fuck.

"Jared was on my case about dating again. I told him I was seeing someone else. He didn't believe me and I was just so sick and tired of his bitching, so I told him I was meeting my date at the party. That turned into me walking up to a stranger and pretending he was my date. Thank goodness he was kind enough to play along with it."

She laughs. "So Mr. Hottie agreed to pretend to be dating you. Maybe he *is* interested in dating you." She wiggles her eyebrows at me.

"He probably thinks I'm crazy or a loser after last night," I grumble.

I don't hate the idea of dating Xavier, but after last night, I'm sure he finds me certifiable.

"He left the party with you right?"

"Yeah. He offered to walk me home."

"See, maybe he was into you."

"I don't know, the whole thing was crazy. And I can't even blame alcohol because I hadn't even drunk anything."

She whistles. "You know how to go big, babe."

"I know, right? Now Jared is going to be hounding me about him, and what can I even say? Pretend I'm still dating him when I'm sure he will turn the other way anytime we meet?"

"I don't know why you put up with Jared's bullshit." Rebecca shakes her head.

My heart pangs. "You know why."

She rolls her eyes. "I get it, but eventually that conversation needs to happen."

"I know," I sigh loudly. "Not yet though. Change of subject, what kind of trouble did you stir up last night?"

CHAPTER TWO

Xavier

I can't get her out of my head.

Cassandra.

It was refreshing to meet such an honest girl so comfortable with herself. I'm kicking myself for not asking for her number, but I thought that would be creepy.

It's probably for the best. She has some unresolved issues with the asshole from the party, anyway. Best not to get myself caught up in that drama. Been there, done that.

"Hey man, I saw you leave the party with little Cassandra Davis," Jack says as he comes back into our shared room.

I let her name roll around in my head. Cassandra Davis. It suits her. I wonder how many Cassandra Davis' there are on social media.

Shaking my head. "Yeah, I walked her home," I say noncommittally as I continue reading my textbook.

"She's been marked off-limits by Jared. You might have some issues there."

I glance up at him. "I can handle myself. Besides, there's nothing there."

"Uh-huh. She's not some smoking hot blonde with legs for days, an ass that you could live off of, and a chest that makes grown men weep."

I chuckle. "She's hot, but I don't think any woman's worth the drama."

"No matter what you say, he thinks you're hitting that. He was beyond pissed after you left with her."

I shrug. "Not my problem what he believes."

"Right," he says. "We're going to Saddle Up Saloon tonight. You in?"

"Sure. Why not?" I tell him.

Last night wasn't overly exciting, but I can't keep cooping myself up in this room. Jack's been a good friend so far.

Or maybe Cassandra will be there.

"Great. We are leaving at seven. If you've got a fake ID, bring it. They won't serve you without it."

I shake my head. "How about I drive and be your DD?"

"My brother. We can take my car though in case I need to get my dick wet, which we both know I will." He smirks.

"With a mouth like that, I can't possibly see how a woman can turn you down," I deadpan.

"Right? The ladies love them some Jack."

"Whatever, man. Now shut up, I need to finish these assignments if you want me to go anywhere."

"Man, you study too much. You need to lighten up."

I don't respond as he grabs a couple of things before leaving.

He doesn't get it. He doesn't have parents like mine. His mom calls him on Sundays and fusses over him and if he's happy. His father talks football with him and asks how his training is going, but never once asks him about his grades.

My parents? I'm lucky if I hear from my mother outside of holidays and my father would kill me if I got anything less than an A.

There are only a couple of routes you can go as a Walsh man. Lawyer, doctor, or businessman. He was pissed when he found out I wanted to teach.

I haven't heard from him since I declared my major. I don't give a fuck though.

At least that's what I tell myself.

I haven't forgiven him for trying to push me on Tinsley last year or the deal he made with her father, but the need to impress him is ingrained in my system. The thought of disappointing him still makes my skin itch.

Hours later, Jack comes back, finding me in the same position I was in with a different textbook when he left.

"Okay, man. Studying is done. We're going to get food, then I'm going to get blitzed. You ready?"

"Yeah, man." I shut my textbook, getting up to pull a T-shirt on.

I slip on my shoes and grab my wallet.

We make our way to his truck, a single cab old Chevy that has seen better days.

Another big difference I've seen in Texas. No one drives the flashy cars I'm used to. Even if they have money to buy a new one, they stick with their old trucks instead.

I asked Jack about his truck once. He said it was a family heirloom, passed down from his grandfather, to his father, and now to him. He said he wouldn't dream of buying a new one.

"Run it 'til the wheels fall off," were his exact words.

It's such a different mentality, but one that's slowly growing on me. I don't feel the pressure to prove my worth based on what I wear or drive. Or how much is in my father's bank account.

It's refreshing. No one cares who I am or who my father is. Jack isn't friends with me because of the perks he can get from me.

He's just a chill guy who has taken me under his wing because I'm his roommate.

He thinks I'm the poor one.

He said that to me once, actually. I tried to buy him dinner, and he said that I didn't have to do that around here. No one cares what money I have.

That I might be rich beyond my wildest dreams, but if I didn't have good friends and a good family life, then I was the poor one.

Then he paid for my dinner.

It was an interesting experience, that's for sure.

We pull up to a diner and make our way inside, getting seated right away.

After we order, Jack talks about school.

"Man, there's this hot as fuck chick in my Lit class that's feisty as fuck. She won't give me the time of day, but fuck if I don't want her, anyway. I can't go there though."

"Yeah? Why not?" I ask.

"She's the take-home-to-mama type, and that's a step I'm not sure I'm ready to take. My mama would love her, though."

I chuckle. "Life's not all about chasing tail. You know that, right?"

"I know, but after Christy-Lynn broke my heart in the tenth grade, I'm not sure I'm ready to risk it again."

"Ah, so you have woman drama. Here I thought you've always been a player," I tease.

"Not at all. I used to be a good, wholesome boy. Then that jezebel went and ruined that. Haven't been the same since."

"That's deep, man," I deadpan, making us laugh.

"Shut up. We both know there's some Christy-Lynn in your past too." He pauses. "Or was it a Bubba?"

I throw a napkin at him. "You're fucked in the head."

"I know, but people love me anyway."

Jack's not wrong. He might not be the good wholesome boy of his past, but he's a good guy. Even with all the playing he does.

"Hey, man. Your girl's here."

My head swings to where he's looking outside.

Cassandra's outside, arguing with the guy from the party. Something inside me urges me to move. To go out there and protect her, but I fight it. It's not my battle.

"Not my girl, man," is all I say to Jack as the waitress brings us our food.

I keep my eye on them as we eat, noticing the moment she walks away and gets in a car with a group of people.

My chest doesn't feel lighter until I see her leave.

"That looked intense," Jack says.

The guy's still standing outside, his fists clenched, looking pissed.

I shrug, not making a comment.

We finish eating, paying the bill, and make our way to the bar. After a quick five-minute drive, we walk through the door, me with big black X's on the back of my hand, Jack hands me his keys.

"I'll let you know if I end up going home with someone else."

I nod, taking in the surrounding scene.

I've been to posh clubs in New York and Chicago. The ones with VIP areas overflowing with champagne and liquor. Bass bumping to the latest rap songs as the girls dance like strippers with barely-there clothing.

Saddle Up Saloon couldn't be further from that. Instead, it's a rustic-looking bar with neon signs peppered throughout. There are bars on either side and a large dance floor in the middle, surrounded by a half wall just wide enough to set your drinks on. There are a couple of pool tables in the corner and a large mechanical bull in another with a chick wearing jean shorts and a plaid button-up tied at her stomach holding on like she's riding for her life.

Instead of rap music, country blares from the speakers as both men and women are on the floor stepping in sync to a dance they all know.

There are a couple of girls wearing short dresses meant for the clubs I'm used to, but most of them are wearing different versions of the girl on the bull's outfit, all with cowgirl boots adorning their feet. I haven't seen one pair of heels yet.

"Come on, man, stop staring at the grits and let's get a drink," Jack says, jostling my shoulder.

"Grits? Like the food?" I reply, thinking of the food Jack forced me to try when I first got here.

It wasn't bad per se, but it was not something I would willingly order on my own.

"Yeah. Girls raised in the south. It's how we breed them down here. They're sexy as fuck, but cross one and next thing you know, your car's keyed. Mine can take it, but your pretty ride might not."

I push his shoulder. "Shut up, man."

Getting a soda for me and a whiskey for him, we make our way to the edge of the dance floor. A different song comes on and my eyes are drawn to the couples on the floor. They dance with each other around the edge of the dance floor, all once again making the same steps. All except one couple.

Cassandra.

I think I could recognize her gorgeous head of hair anywhere now.

She's in the arms of a much older man; he twirls her around the dance floor. Doing complicated steps I couldn't even begin to do.

As they fly by us, I hear her laughter, bringing a smile to my face.

She looks like she's having the time of her life.

"You gonna let that man handle your girl like that?" Jack jokes.

I smile, deciding then and there. This is the third time I've seen her since last night. I'm taking it as a sign. I'm going to get her phone number tonight.

Cassi

THIS ISN'T HOW I wanted my day to go.

I woke up this morning thinking about Xavier.

Scratch that, I dreamt of Xavier and his large hands all over me amongst other parts of his body.

It left me feeling this high I haven't felt in a really long fucking time when I woke up. I was on cloud nine, thinking about how I could run into him again.

Then I checked my phone and deflated.

Eleven messages, all from Jared.

I ignored them all and went about my day, excited to be going to my favorite country bar tonight, but then he found me at dinner.

The look on his face when I told him I needed space still haunts me.

"I need you, Cassi," Jared pleads.

My heart hurt for him. He's still so lost while I'm moving on. I don't know how to help him.

First thing I did when I got to Saddle Up was find Virgil. He always brightens my day.

"You ready?" he asks as he leads me to the dance floor.

"Never been more ready. Are you? You're not getting any younger," I tease.

"I still got moves, young lady. Don't you worry about that."

Next thing I know, we're moving. I love dancing with Virgil. I let go of everything and let him lead. He makes me feel as if I'm floating on air as he moves me around the dance floor, adding spins, twisting me to his will.

I can't help but laugh as we dance.

I love when his face lights up. He enjoys dancing as much as I enjoy dancing with him.

At the end of the song, we're both out of breath. He kisses my hand, going back to his spot, waiting for the next girl who wants to dance. And there's never a shortage.

I know I'll be back in that line before the end of the night.

Making my way back to Mara, I smile as she hands me water.

"Thanks," I breathe out before taking a long drink.

I'm not old enough to drink, but even if I was, I don't drink anymore.

Never since that night.

Shaking my demons away, I smile as Mara drones on about some guy she spotted already.

"You're such a hussy." I smile.

"Hey, I'm just playing the game. Who says the guys get to be the only players?"

"Touché."

"Well, hello there, girlfriend," he says from behind me.

I know I only met him last night, but I swear I could recognize his voice anywhere.

A deep, warm tone that warms up the ice that formed a year ago.

Turning, I smile as I see the same black X's on his hands.

"Hi, boyfriend. What are you doing here?"

He shrugs. "Stalking my girlfriend while she dances with other men."

We both laugh as Mara watches on with interest.

"Virgil's harmless. He's like sixty. Although, he is a fantastic dancer." I take a sip of my water to hide my smile.

"I don't know about him, but you looked damn good out there."

"It's all Virgil. Him and his wife used to dance all the time. When she passed, he kept coming and dancing with anyone who would ask. Before long, he kind of became a local attraction. As long as you can let him lead, he can make you look like you've been dancing for years. You have to catch him before he leaves, though. He only stays until eleven. After that, they stop playing two-step music and start playing music to cater to the younger crowd."

His smile grows as I talk. "I'll keep that in mind in case I ever want to dance with Virgil," he teases, making me roll my eyes.

Mara clears her throat.

Turning to her, I shoot her a 'shut up' look.

She ignores it, inserting herself next to Xavier. "Hi, I'm Mara, Cassi's best friend."

He shakes her hand, but quickly lets go, returning his attention to me. "I'm Xavier."

"Ah, the fake boyfriend," Mara says as she lays her hand on his arm.

He moves away from her, closer to me, making me smile.

"That's what I've been told," he responds.

"Well," she says as she grabs her drink. "I think I need to go find me a cowboy to ride. If you two will excuse me."

As she walks off, he turns to me. "She's interesting."

I chuckle. "Yeah, she's something else."

"So, I don't want this to seem awkward, but can I get your number?" He rubs the back of his head, like he's nervous.

I smile sweetly at him. "That depends."

"On what?" He quirks his brow at me.

"What are you planning to do with it?" I ask, biting my lip.

His eyes follow the movement, darkening with lust. "I thought maybe we could be friends."

My elation at him asking for my number deflates as he says the dreaded F-word.

Of course he wants to be friends.

I've never been overly girly. Not really the type guys want to date. More like one of the guys.

"Sure, I could always use friends." I force a smile, reaching my hand out for his phone.

When he places it in my hands, I don't miss the shock I get as his skin touches mine.

I quickly type my phone number in, saving it as Just A Friend to be cheeky. Then I close out of the contacts and hand it back.

"Thanks," he says, settling in to hang out.

"Anytime." I turn to the table, setting my water down.

The conversation's stilted, neither of us sure what to say.

Then the next song comes on and I smile.

"Do you mind watching my drink? I love this dance."

He gives me a flirty smile. "Do I get to watch you dance?"

That warm feeling is back. He's flirting with me. I kind of like it. "You can watch all you want, friend."

He winces, but laughs as I stroll away, finding my spot on the dance floor.

As I move with the rest of the crowd, I feel his eyes on me. Almost like they are burning a hole into my skin. I don't know why, but with him watching me, it makes me want to do better. Swivel my hips sexier. Kick higher. It's empowering knowing he was watching me.

I stay out for three songs before coming back to find him with a fresh glass of water next to him.

"You didn't poison it, did you?"

He laughs. "You trusted me to watch your drink, but you don't trust a new one?"

"Fair point. Thank you."

"You're welcome." He smirks, taking a drink of his own water. "So Cassandra, what made you decide to come out tonight?"

"You can call me Cassi since we're friends and all," I tease. "Not much to do around here. Same ol' stuff, different podunk town, so why not go dancing?"

"I wouldn't call Carver podunk. I've driven through some small towns. And last I checked, over thirty thousand residents isn't podunk."

I take a second to think. "True. I guess I feel like it's confining because I've only ever lived here. I haven't traveled much."

"You grew up in Lubbock?"

"Well, close enough. I'm from Ropesville. It's about thirty minutes outside of here. Get too far off this main area and there's nothing but steers and ranches."

"Not going to lie, I can't imagine living like that, but it sounds pretty awesome. I've lived in cities most of my life. The hustle gets real old real quick. When I was younger, I thought it was glamorous, but now it's…." He trails off.

"Too much?"

"Impersonal? It feels impersonal. Not like here. I feel like every person I meet wants to be my friend. It's a different atmosphere completely."

I chuckle. "Good ol' small town USA. Where your neighbor treats you like you're his next of kin. Hell, he might be."

"Like one big happy family, huh?"

"Something like that. At least we aren't somewhere like Alabama, where to get married you have to take a DNA test to prove you aren't related," I say, making him laugh.

I shake my head. "I'm being serious. It could be worse."

"Well, fuck. That's kind of creepy." He cringes.

"Don't worry, city boy. No way you're related to any of my kin. Not with style like that," I tease.

"Thank god for small favors." He winks.

My watch vibrates, making me look down.

Timer: time to head home.

I sigh. Just when things were getting started.

"Everything okay?"

"Yeah, I just need to head back to the dorms." I look around, trying to find Mara. "Looks like I need to find a new ride," I murmur, watching her make-out with some guy on the dance floor.

"How about I drive you back," Xavier offers.

"Are you sure? What about Jack?"

"He will find a different ride home. If not, I can always come back and grab him."

"If you're sure, I would appreciate it."

Xavier stands, taking his phone out of his pocket. I check my pockets, making sure I have everything I need. I shoot off a text to Mara, letting her know I'm leaving.

"There, I texted him and told him I was heading out. You ready?"

"Yeah." I smile.

Xavier rests his hand on my lower back, walking me out. Once outside, the cool air makes me shiver.

"You cold?" he rasps, leading me toward an old truck.

"No, I just didn't realize how hot I was until we got out here."

He opens the passenger door for me, letting me jump in before shutting it. I watch as he rounds the hood of the truck, sliding in. The truck starts off with a rumble as we buckle our seat belts.

"So, this isn't what I pictured you driving," I say as he pulls out of the parking lot, heading toward campus.

"No?" He smiles. "What did you think I would drive?"

"I don't know, a BMW," I say, making him laugh.

"Nah, I don't own a BMW. I have a Maserati, this is Jack's truck."

"That makes more sense." I nod.

Before I know it we're pulling up in front of my door.

"Well, thank you for dropping me off," I say as I unbuckle my seat belt.

"It's no problem," Xavier says, undoing his belt.

"What are you doing?" I frown.

"Just stay there." He jumps out of the truck, running around the hood, and opens my door for me.

Has a guy ever opened my door for me not once but twice in one night? I mean you would think so seeing as I live in Texas, but those ways seem to have died out with my generation.

"Thank you," I mumble, getting out.

"You're welcome."

I lean up, brushing my lips against his cheek. His stubble grazing my lips. "Have a good night."

"You too."

I walk around him, heading toward my building. Peeking over my shoulder, I see him standing there leaning against the hood of the truck, watching me.

Walking backward, I yell, "What are you doing?"

"Making sure you get inside the building okay!" he hollers back, making me smile.

I turn, walking up the steps. Gripping the door handle, I yell back, "Night!"

"Night."

As I walk toward my room, all I can think about is how dangerous a guy like him could be.

CHAPTER THREE

Xavier

"What are your plans for this weekend?" Jack asks.

I shrug. "Nothing planned really. Thought I might see if Cassi wanted to hang."

"Cassi, huh?" He wiggles his brows at me.

"It's not like that. She's a really chill girl who's fun to hang out with."

"Sure. It doesn't hurt that she has a nice rack either."

I toss a pillow at him.

He holds up his hands. "Hey. Didn't know you were that into her."

"I'm not. It's not like that. We're friends."

He sits down on his bed facing me. "Listen, you keep telling yourself that, but let me give you a warning. Cassi seems like one of them girls."

"One of what girls?"

He chuckles. "I forget you're a city boy. We call girls like Cassi, one of them girls. She's down to earth, can hang with the boys, and is just as likely to chop your balls off than kiss you. She's a pistol, that's for sure, but when you get you one of them girls? It's done. Game over. They are the type you would be stupid not to marry. Especially if she gives you the time of day. Cassi is one of them girls."

"That's a lot of thinking for you, bud. Your brain okay over there?" I joke.

He shakes his head, standing to go to his dresser. "Laugh it up, X. Those girls are once in a lifetime. Meet them at the wrong time and you could miss out on the best thing in your life. I hope I don't meet one of them girls until I'm at least thirty. I want to sow my wild oats. Feel my freedom. Don't get locked down by one of them girls, X. Don't do it."

"You're reading way too much into this. Cassi's just a friend. I'm not looking for anything right now."

"Sure. Whatever you say. I'll be at the bar if you need me."

With that, he leaves.

Picking up my phone, I call Cassi.

"Hey, what's up?" Her voice comes over the phone.

"Nothing much. How was your day?" I ask.

"Good. Classes droned on forever. I'm so glad it's Friday."

"Same. What are you up to this weekend?"

"Tonight I'm watching movies with Mara. Then tomorrow I'm going on a hike, so I'll probably crash early tomorrow night. Why? What's up?"

"Nothing. Hiking, huh? You're not scared of bugs and snakes?" I tease.

She chuckles. "Hell no. I can handle myself with a few forest critters. Maybe if a bear came along, it would worry."

I shake my head, laughing. "Of course. You can take on the world."

"Damn right. I may be five-foot-five, but I pack a mean punch."

"Okay, Rocky Balboa. Calm down over there. Where are you going hiking?"

"Why do you want to know? You planning on stalking me? I mean, I know I'm hot shit, but that doesn't warrant light stalking."

"Ha. You wish. I'm just wondering where in the great state of Texas there are any mountains. I've only seen desert and city since I've been here."

"Of course you have. You haven't ventured off the beaten path. How about this? No stalking required. I officially invite you to go hiking with me tomorrow."

"Sure. I'm down."

"You realize I'm leaving at five in the morning."

"I'm a morning person. It's no problem."

She chuckles. "Don't you go out buying new hiking boots and shit tonight. You'll regret it tomorrow. Wear something comfortable. It gets hot quick. I'll make sure I have everything you need. What size shoe do you wear?"

"Whoa there. I don't reveal that until the second date," I tease.

"You're so stupid. I might have a pair of broken-in boots for you. What size?"

"Twelve and a half. Where are you getting these boots?"

"Don't you worry about that. It might be a tight squeeze, but I think I have a pair I can borrow."

"That's a little weird, but thanks, I guess?"

"You'll be thanking me tomorrow. Five a.m. sharp, Xavier. Don't be late. Meet me here and we can take my car."

"I can drive."

She chuckles again. "Trust me. You want me to drive. See you in the morning."

"Later."

I toss my phone on my desk and can't help but smile.

Looks like I'm going hiking.

"Wow, COLOR ME impressed." Cassie stands next to her car as I get out of mine.

"What?" I ask.

"You're here five minutes early. Going for extra points?"

"I honestly was about twenty minutes early, but didn't want to wake you or your roommate in case you were still in bed."

She narrows her eyes. "Do you think I'm not a morning person?"

I laugh. "I think mornings are not a close friend of yours."

She glares, but it turns into a small smile. "We haven't always been on the best of terms. You really like mornings?"

I shrug. "It's not about liking it. I'm just used to it."

"I don't think I could ever get used to waking up this early, but every once in a while I can do it. Let's get going before it gets too light."

"Where are we going, anyway?"

"You'll see."

We get into her car and get on the road.

"So you like hiking and dancing. What else is there to know about you?" I ask to fill the silent car.

"Coffee. I need coffee before I can take too much talky. We're stopping by the diner to get some."

"Coffee it is." I try to suppress my laugh.

"Laugh all you want, Avi. You won't be laughing when I bite your head off because I haven't had my coffee."

"Avi?"

"Shhhh."

We make it to the diner in five minutes and get our coffee and a couple of breakfast sandwiches to go. Once back in the car, she blows on her coffee before taking a large sip.

"Heaven. This is heaven."

"Can we talk now or am I still in the danger zone?"

She takes another long sip. "Now you may talk."

"Why thank you, your majesty," I jest.

"That's right, loyal subject. Bow to the queen of crazy."

"I don't think you're crazy."

"All women are crazy. It's what level of crazy that you need to worry about."

"Ah, so I should be worried I got in a car with the queen then."

"That's right. Maybe I'm actually planning to drive you out to the desert to murder you and defile your corpse before leaving you to the vultures."

"Oh. Wow. Drink more coffee. You're not you when you're cranky," I tease.

"Watch it, Avi. It's still early."

"Where did this new nickname for me come from?"

She shrugs. "Xavier's a lot to say. I think it's cute. Avi. Rolls of the tongue."

"I don't think I've ever had anyone call me that."

She glances at me with a smile. "Good. It's just for me then."

"Well, shit. I feel like I should have a special nickname for you now. Cass? Dra? Dre?"

She bursts out laughing. "A lot of people call me Cass. Dra? Really? Dre doesn't even make sense."

"Sorry, I'm not quite creative as you."

"What about Adra?"

She laughs. "Whatever you want, Avi."

"Adra it is. My own special nickname for you. I better not hear your friends calling you this."

"I can assure you no one has ever called me Adra. It's all yours."

"Great. Now that we have that settled, how about telling me where we are going?"

"Nice try. It's not a long drive. We will be there soon."

"How's rooming with Jack?" she asks.

"Good, I like him. He's a good dude. Do you like your roommate?" I trail off.

"Rebecca." She nods. "She's one of my best friends. We grew up together. Like spending every weekend together at one of our houses. So it made sense when we came to the same college. We knew we could live together without jeopardizing our relationship."

"What about Mara? She said she was your best friend, right?" I ask.

"Her mom and mine are best friends, so we grew up together. But I'm closer to Rebecca."

"That's cool. I moved so much that I never really got to build relationships like that." I shift uncomfortably in my seat.

"Yeah, but I bet you've been to some pretty cool places."

"I have," I say thoughtfully.

"Well, don't hold back now," she teases, making me laugh.

I launch into telling her about Paris, England, Dubai, and more. One story after another. Describing each place. From the people, the food, and the culture.

I watch how the plains turn into valleys, then rock cliffs, and into desolate mountains.

Wouldn't want to get lost out here.

"Here we are. Welcome to Guadalupe Mountains National Park."

"I've never heard of this place," I murmur to myself.

"I don't think most people know about it unless they are from Texas." She shrugs. "Come on, let's grab our packs." Cassi hops out of the car, popping the trunk. I follow, looking around.

"It's so dry."

"That's why we have plenty of water, city boy." Cassi smirks. "Here, try these on." She points to a pair of boots in the trunk.

"Where are we hiking?" I ask, ignoring her jest. Grabbing the boots, I open the back door of her car and slip off my shoes, trading them for the boots.

"We are going up to Guadalupe Peak," she says sliding her pack into place. "How do the boots feel?"

"I should be good," I say, standing, testing the boots out. "How high?"

"It's a little under nine thousand feet above sea level. We should be good."

Shutting the door, I grab the second pack, tossing it onto my back. "Lead the way." I wave, letting her walk in front of me.

Cassi

I DON'T KNOW what I was thinking when I invited Xavier to hike with me. I'm attracted to him, which should be my first red flag. I don't need to be getting into any more complicated relationships.

My second red flag? He's actually funny. He's kind and considerate. He's what I would normally look for in a man.

Maybe that's why I'm gravitating toward him. He makes me feel things I haven't felt in a while. He makes me feel more like the old me. He makes me feel like I'm more than this one event in my life.

A pang in my chest hits me as I watch him pull Ryan's old hiking boots on. Ryan liked to hike with me. I haven't had the urge to bring anyone else with me since he passed. Even though Jared hiked with us from time to time, I couldn't bear going with him now.

Yet yesterday when Xavier called, I smiled. When he teased me, I laughed. Not a forced laugh, but a genuine laugh. Then, before I knew it, I was inviting him with me.

Let's not talk about the ride here. I don't know why I called him Avi, but it stuck. I didn't lie to him. It's easier to say, and it's a cute nickname. What I didn't tell him is that it makes him hotter.

Maybe that's why butterflies swarmed my stomach when he said only I've ever called him that. Or why my heart raced when he picked out his own nickname for me. One that's only his.

"How long is this hike and do we have a game plan?" he asks, pulling me out of my head.

I shake my head and say over my shoulder. "Don't get killed. I don't have a very solid alibi."

"True. I did leave my car at your place and I told Jack and Tinsley I was going hiking with you."

"Tinsley?" I frown.

"My best friend from back home," he says, falling into step with me.

"Ah. The infamous best friend from the video message." I can't deny the pang of jealousy that hits me.

"Don't worry. You're my only Adra. So this way?"

He breaks off, heading in the wrong direction.

"You're going to get lost. This way, dummy." I point toward the sign, telling us where to go.

"Ah that's what those signs are."

I smack his arm, taking up the lead. "Don't stare at my ass."

"Wouldn't dream of it," he says, but as I peek back, he's totally staring at my ass.

He glances up and gives me a cheeky smile. "Sorry. It's like it's the Earth and I'm the moon. I can't help but gravitate around it."

"That was cheesy as fuck." I face forward.

"Cheesy, but you liked it."

"Not at all," I say, hiding the smile on my face.

Xavier

I FOLLOW CASSI up the trail, watching her ass sway side to side.

Do not pop a boner, do not pop a boner.

"So tell me something about you."

"What do you want to know?"

"What are you majoring in?" she asks, looking over her shoulder.

"I'm going for my teaching degree. I want to work with kids."

"Really?" I hear the skepticism in her voice.

"Really."

"Uh." She turns around, walking backward as she looks at me. "I can see it." She nods. "You'd be the hot teacher all the high school girls want." She winks, turning around.

"Yeah, because that's what I was shooting for." We both laugh. "What about you?" I ask.

"I'm undecided, much to my parents' dismay." She sighs. "I don't know why they think I should decide now."

"At least your family is okay with whatever you choose. My father is currently in denial and thinks I will switch to a business degree like he wants," I say bitterly.

"Don't want to run the family business?"

"Not at all." I shake my head adamantly. "What about you?"

Cassi shrugs. "I could see myself living on a ranch. Working with horses and cattle. Is it what I want? I'm not sure. But I like the option to pursue something else."

"I could see it," I say, picturing her working with animals and living off the land.

"What made you choose teaching?" she asks, taking the attention off of herself.

"I'm sure you've heard the story before. There was a teacher when I was younger who listened, helped. Made me want to help the next generation."

"Come on, it's not that generic. Tell me the entire story."

I let out a deep sigh. "Honestly? I didn't even know what I wanted to be. Not even back then. I've always been groomed to take over Dad's import and export business. Then, in the eighth grade, I met Mr. Roberts. He was a strict guy, but fair. He was never mean, just firm. Always pushing his students to be the best versions of themselves. I guess that's where it started. I watched how he was. The way he could care for so many students at once. You could tell he cared too. No matter how many times a kid caught an attitude with him or how many jokes they made, he never gave up on them. I guess I realized that's what I wished my father were like. It didn't happen right away. I didn't leave his class deciding to become a teacher. That was later when I realized if I continued to let my father lead my life the way he wanted, I would be miserable. So I thought about what I wanted to do. What would make me happy? That's when I thought of Mr. Roberts. I realized what would make me happy is to do everything I can to help the next generation. So I came here."

"That's admirable you know." She looks back over her shoulder, raising a brow.

"If you say so." I huff, feeling the strain of the hike set in.

"So your father doesn't approve?"

"He thinks this is some sort of rebellion against him. He is hoping that I decide to change majors. Honestly, the only reason he hasn't cut me off completely is because of his image. In order to save face, he has to at least pretend to support me. Can't let his associates see him disown me."

"If that's the case, why do you still use his money? I don't mean that as an insult, but you could really make it on your own."

I give her a sad smile. "If only it were that easy. This is really hard for me to admit, but I'm accustomed to having money. I mean before Jack I didn't even know you could have friends who didn't care about your money. Well, and Tinsley, but she had more money than I did. I guess, the simple answer is I'm scared."

She pats my shoulder. "That's brave of you to admit. It's okay. You'll get there. So tell me about what kind of trouble a young Avi got into," she teases.

I tell her all about my childhood, her telling me about hers. The rest of the hike we keep to lighter subjects. Our likes and dislikes and before I know it we're cresting the top of the mountain. Walking toward the edge of the mountain, we look below. Solid red rocky cliffs surrounding us as we look down into the valley. It's desolate and makes you feel so small.

"It's beautiful in a way only a desert can be," she murmurs.

"I honestly don't think I've ever seen anything like it."

"I packed some trail mix and whatnot for us. We should eat some and hydrate before we start back down," Cassi says as she pulls her pack off. "I put some snacks in the outside pocket. I figured when we hit the first town, we can grab some food."

"Thanks."

"You're welcome." She shrugs. "I invited you, the least I could do is make sure you have something to munch on."

Sitting on the ground, we snack as we point out different things we see. Once done, we put our trash back into our packs.

"Ready?" Cassi asks as she brushes her butt off.

Without thinking, I pull my phone out and snap a picture of her. Her hair all over the place, making her look like a beautiful mess.

"Hey." She frowns.

"What? I like taking pictures of beautiful things." I shrug, taking a photo of the view.

She slowly approaches. "Well then, how about a photo together? To remember this by."

I pull her into my side, wrapping my arm around her shoulders.

"Say cheese," I tell her, snapping a photo of the two of us.

CHAPTER FOUR

Cassi

Headphones in, head down, I run through the study guide the professor gave the class. I don't know why, but for some reason, math makes my head spin and I rather do anything else instead of trying to figure out algebra. It didn't make sense in high school, and it definitely doesn't make sense now.

Dropping the sheet, I cover my face, groaning in frustration.

Would getting a tutor help?

How will I ever pass this class?

Maybe I can find someone to do it for me.

Uncovering my face, I take a deep breath and pick the sheet back up.

You can do this.

"Boo," he rasps in my ear, making me jump.

"What the hell, Avi," I whisper-shout, slapping his shoulder. Xavier laughs, sliding into the seat next to me.

"What are you doing?" he asks, making himself comfortable.

"What does it look like?" I grumble.

"Considering you're in a library and look frustrated, I would say school work." He smirks, picking up the paper I dropped. "College algebra?"

"Yeah," I say, rubbing my temples.

"College algebra should be pretty much the same across the board, right?"

"Probably." I frown, wondering where he's going with this.

"When's it due?" His eyes focus on the paper.

"Thursday," I tell him.

"Well, how about I keep this." He waves the paper back and forth. "And I'll look over it. Then I will help you out."

"Really?" I say skeptically.

"Really. I won't do it for you, but I will help you learn the material."

"Thank you," I whisper, running my finger on the edge of the table, unable to look him in the eye.

"Hey," he says softly, tugging on the ends of my hair. I look up and see him biting his lip. "You want to get out of here?"

"That sounds awesome."

Xavier watches me pack up my belongings before resting his hand on my lower back and walking me out of the library.

Once outside. he turns. "What would you like to do?" he asks, shoving his hands into his pockets.

"What would you normally be doing if you hadn't invited me out?"

"Playing video games with Jack."

"Oooh. Let's do that. It sounds fun."

"Really?" he says skeptically.

"Yep. Loser buys pizza."

"I'm game. Let me call Jack and have him meet us at the dorm."

He dials Jack as he leads me to his car.

"Hey, you at the dorm?"

I smile as I hear Jack's voice on the phone. I can't hear the words, but his tone always makes me smile. He has an infectious smile, and the boy is never serious.

"Cassi and I are joining you. We will be there in ten. For the love of God man, pick your drawers up off the floor."

He clicks the phone off as he opens the passenger door for me. Then he rounds the front of the car, jumping in.

"I'm surprised you want to play video games with us. Usually girls hate that kind of thing."

I watch as he turns out of the parking lot, staying quiet for a moment.

Then, I turn to look at the side of his face. He is handsome. Even with his city boy style, I can't deny I'm attracted to him.

Maybe this is a bad idea.

I brush the thought away.

"I'm not a normal girl. I think you'll find we are a different breed down here."

He chuckles. "You're right. It's a whole different world down here."

"What do you think of it?" I ask, realizing I never asked him if he even liked it here.

He glances my way, smiling. "It's interesting. The people are different. Jack, for example, is a goofball, but he's loyal as fuck. I've never had that for myself before."

"Jack's a special one."

"It's not just him, though. The people here are friendlier. Do you know how many times people wave at me or even give me a simple smile?"

"Oh yeah, I'm sure the girls are falling all over you," my sarcastic tone hides the twinge of jealousy that I feel when I think about it.

What the fuck is that? I think to myself.

"Sure. The girls are friendly, but it's not just them. Everyone has been very hospitable to me. It's a different experience."

"You make it sound like people are assholes where you're from."

"Maybe not assholes, per se. Disconnected is the word I would use. Here, everyone is in your business. Where I'm from, people won't even make eye contact with you on the streets. They are so focused on their own lives that they don't even look around."

"That sounds bleak."

"You can see why Texas is refreshing for me. So you want to play video games? That's crazy to me. I'm used to girls that care more about taking their next selfie or shopping than spending quality time together."

"Quality time, huh? Is that what we're calling it?"

He smiles at me. "Yep. Quality time. Besides, you can learn a lot about a person from the way they play video games."

"Oh yeah? What are you hoping to learn about me?"

He doesn't look at me, but I can see the side of his lip tick up. "Everything."

My heart races.

Why do I want him to know everything?

"There's not that much to learn."

"I think there's more to you than you let on. It's okay though. I'm patient."

When he pulls into his parking spot, he gets out.

I don't move to follow him right away, attempting to fight the sudden blush covering my face.

Friends. We are friends.

He opens the door, reaching his hand in to help me out.

As soon as I slip my hand into his, a spark lights me up. My breath catches as my heart beats faster and I feel flutters in my stomach.

He gives me a smirk like he knows what just happened, but how could he?

How could he know that for the first time in a long time I feel something other than overwhelming grief?

"Come on," he lets go of my hand, breaking the connection.

I follow him inside, barely containing myself from reaching out to touch him again. To feel that feeling again.

He opens the door to his dorm, ushering me inside before closing it behind him.

I stop, taking in his room. There's a window along the far wall with the blinds closed. On each side of the room is a bed. To the right, the bedding is messed up like someone had just woken up. To the left, the bed is made and looks immaculate. In the middle of the room, there are two beanbag chairs. Straight ahead, there is a TV on a dresser in front of the window. Jack is sitting in one of the chairs, playing a game.

"That game looks interesting," I murmur, knowing full well what game he is playing.

"Let me finish this game and X and I will teach you how to play." Jack says.

I let a smirk fill my face.

They are falling for it. Hook, line, and sinker.

Tonight is going to be interesting.

Xavier

WE WALK INTO my dorm to find Jack already playing a solo game in front of the TV we have set up.

It was a short ride, but it was deeper than I expected. I hadn't expected to open up to this girl the way I have, but fuck if it doesn't feel good.

I mean some of the shit I've told her, I haven't even told Tinsley. I was always careful with Tinsley, making sure she was okay. She had her own shit going on and didn't need mine.

I feel like Cassi has her own shit going on too, but with her, I feel like it's okay to deal with my shit too. Like we can work through it together.

Fuck if that doesn't feel refreshing.

Cassi's eyes take in our dorm. It's not much to look at, but it still makes me anxious.

I want her to like my space.

"That game looks interesting," Cassi smirks.

"Let me finish this game and X and I will teach you how to play."

"Avi and I have a bet." I smile as she uses the nickname she's given me. "Whoever loses buys pizza. You in?"

Jack laughs. "Totally. Better be ready to pay up, sweet cheeks."

I smack him across the back of the head. "Watch it."

He chuckles. "No harm, no foul. Right, Cass?"

"Not at all. Now, what do these buttons do?" She holds up the controller.

She takes a seat on the vacant bean bag chair, leaving me to get on my bed. Not the best vantage point to be playing, but for her, it's worth it.

After a quick lesson, we jump into a three player game. After the first couple minutes, I can see we've been duped.

Cassi's better than we thought. She's really fucking good. It's hot as hell.

"Oh, did I kill you, sugar?" Cassi asks Jack, shooting a wink at me.

"How did you do that?" he grumbles.

"Beginner's luck, I guess. Oops. I did it again."

I chuckle, watching her play more than watching my screen. By the time the round is done, Jack tosses his controller down.

"You sandbagging little jerk. You knew how to play."

She shrugs. "I like ham on my pizza. Ooh, and breadsticks."

"Watch your girl, X. She's a hustler," Jack says as he calls the pizza place to put in our order.

"Where did you learn to play like that?" I turn to face her completely.

"My brother, Ryan. He played a lot when we were growing up. There wasn't much else to do around the ranch, so we often played together. Sometimes with Jared, too. I guess when you spend hours at a time perfecting your skill so the boys don't always slaughter you, it kind of sticks with you."

I laugh. "I would've bought you pizza either way. You know that, right?"

"Yeah, but I feel like Jack needed to be reminded women are more than a nice ass and great rack."

"You're damn right they are. They're a good lay too," he says as he hangs up the phone.

Cassie smacks his arm. "We have brains too you know."

"Oh, I know. I stay away from the smart ones like you, though. You're the ones always wanting the big 'M' word." He shivers. "I'm not ready for that yet."

Cassi laughs. "Big, strong Jack's scared of a little marriage talk, huh? You realize we're in college, right? Not all women are looking to settle down and have kids at twenty."

"What about you?" I ask, not sure why I want to know.

"Hell no. This is my first year in college. I don't even know what I want right now. Marriage and kids? Sure, someday, but not right now. Are you telling me you want that?" she asks wide-eyed.

I shrug. "One day. If I found the right girl."

"Well, I know I can't even think about it without my skin crawling. Hell, I'll probably never get married. Can we drop all this talking bullshit and get back to the game?"

"Jack," I warn.

Cassi laughs. "I thought you would never shut up. Let's get back to me whooping your ass."

As we continue to play, I glance over at Cassi more and more. She's beautiful, sure, but I've never met anyone like her. She has this feisty personality that makes her shine that much brighter. Add in the mouth like a sailor, and she's a catch.

I find myself comparing her to Tinsley. Tinsley's beautiful, with a soul made for a saint. She's always so sweet and forgiving.

I can't imagine her ever wanting to play a video game, let alone owning us guys as she does it.

Tinsley's an angel, but Cassi? She's a firecracker.

"Stop staring at my tits and play the game, Avi," Cassi bumps into me, gaining my attention again.

"Can't help it. Listening to some of those words fly out of your mouth, I had to look to make sure you were real."

"Never heard a woman curse before? Buckle up, buddy. This is going to be a long night."

A long night it is, but I wouldn't trade a minute of it.

Cassi

"COME ON, Z. Up in the bed you go."

I smile and crack my eyes open. "What are you doing?"

Xavier lifts me easily into his arms, standing. He places me on his bed, pulling the blanket over me.

"You fell asleep on the floor. It looked uncomfortable." He brushes a piece of hair away from my face.

I scoot over and pat the spot beside me. It's a twin-size bed, so it will be a squeeze, but fuck if I don't want to get up and go home right now.

"You can take the bed. Don't worry about it. I'll take the floor," Xavier leans down to grab a pillow, but I grab his arm instead, pulling him down next to me.

"We are two adults who are old enough to share a bed. This way, we both get to be comfortable," I reason with him.

"Are you sure? I really can sleep on the floor."

"Stop arguing with me and get in here."

He finally slides under the blanket next to me, but tries to give me space. I squash that real quick, cuddling into his chest. He stiffens.

"You can touch me, you know. I'm not going to melt," I tease.

His hand reluctantly comes to rest on my side.

"There you go," I quip.

He chuckles. "You don't give anyone a break, do you?"

I smile against his chest. "Nope. When you grow up with a brother and his best friend who's there just as much as he is, you learn to get some thick skin. I don't know how to act any other way."

"So you can hang out like just one of the boys?" he asks.

I purse my lips before speaking. "I suppose you could look at it that way. In high school, guys seemed reluctant to date me. Sometimes it was because of my brother, but others I don't think they could handle that I could give as good as I could take."

"It can be intimidating to some guys. Having a woman who can do the things they can do. Let me guess, you can change the oil in your car yourself."

"My car, my parents, the tractor. You name it and I can probably change the oil. Hell, most parts honestly. That's not from being raised with boys, though. That's all my dad. He wanted me to know how to take care of myself. Besides, living on a ranch meant taking care of things yourself. Daddy never hired anyone to come tend to his machinery."

"Fuck, I shouldn't say this while you're in my arms, but you keep getting hotter and hotter."

"Oh, so I don't intimidate you?" I quip.

"You do. For all I know, you're about to chop my dick off or you're about to kiss me, but fuck, that just makes you sexier."

"You say that now, but if you dated me, my mouth would get old real quick."

He pulls back so I tilt my face up to look at him.

"I don't know who you dated in the past, but there's nothing wrong with your mouth. Hell, if I was in a better place mentally, I would do many things with that mouth."

His eyes glance to my lips. My tongue sneaks out, wetting it. I think I hear him mutter something like "fuck it," but I can't be sure because the beating of my heart drowns it out.

Just when our lips are about to meet, a sudden, loud noise in the room startles us a part.

"Fucking gross ass roommate of mine," Xavier mutters.

My hand flies over my mouth as I try to withhold the laughter. "Did he just fart?"

"Yes, that fucking cockblock."

I press my face into his chest as I let the laughter flow. A few seconds later, I feel Xavier's chest shake with his own amusement.

"I think that was a sign we should go to sleep. We have class tomorrow," he says.

"We do," I agree.

He pulls me in closer before whispering in my ear. "'Night, Adra."

"'Night, Avi."

In the warmth of his arms, I allow myself to drift into a peaceful sleep.

⚘

I STARTLE AWAKE at the slamming door.

"Fuck, why are you always so goddamn loud, Jack?" Xavier murmurs into my hair.

I breathe in his scent as I cuddle closer to his chest. I feel completely content as I hear the beating of his heart beneath my ear.

His hand reaches out to run his fingers through my hair.

"Sorry, princess. I didn't realize you still had company. Besides, it's like noon. You should be up by now."

I shoot straight up. "Noon? Fuck, I have to go. I'm going to be late to class."

Xavier chuckles. "Late? Try I missed all of my morning classes."

I wince. "Sorry."

He stands up, watching as I pull my shoes on and grab my bag. "It was worth it."

My belly warms at his words. Missing class was worth it. Does he mean because of me?

Is it wrong that I hope it's because of me?

"I've got to go. Thanks for the video games and pizza. Talk to you later?" I smile up at him.

He leans in, hugging me to his chest before placing a chaste kiss on the top of my head. "Text me when you get out of class."

"Will do. Bye, Jack."

"Yeah, bye Ace."

I smile to myself as I shut the door. Ace. Jack called me that after our fourth round. He said I was an Ace at shooting, then demanded we play teams instead. I think his ego was getting wounded by all the ass-kicking I was doing.

Too bad for him. My brother always taught me to win. Never concede, even if it's to stroke a man's ego.

A pang hits me in my chest.

Ryan.

God, I miss him.

Shaking off my somber thoughts, I head to my room to quickly change. As I open the door, Rebecca accosts me.

"Where have you been, missy? Doing the walk of shame at noon." She tsks her tongue.

"I stayed over with Jack and Xavier," I tell her as I quickly undress before dressing again.

"Two men at a time? Damn, you're such a hussy," she teases.

"Not two men at once, you dumbass. We were playing video games 'til late, and I fell asleep."

She gives me a knowing smirk as I turn to face her. "So whose bed did you end up in?"

Rolling my eyes, I give her a quick hug. "I don't have time for this. I'm already late. See you later!"

I rush out of the room and practically run to humanities. I offer a small smile in apology as slip into class ten minutes late. Thankfully, my professor doesn't stop teaching as I make my way to my seat. Once there, I take a deep breath before pulling out my laptop.

I'm taking notes furiously when my phone vibrates in my pocket. Glancing up at the professor, I take a chance to glance at it quickly.

> **Avi:** You made an impression on Jack. He's been bragging to all the boys about his "Ace".

My heart races. I don't know why he does this to me. Typing out a quick response, I leave my phone on my knee.

> **Me:** Haha. I'm surprised he's telling anyone he got his ass kicked by a girl.
> **Avi:** Oh, he isn't telling them who Ace is. He is, however, signing you up for a tournament with all the guys and betting his basket on you.

I smile. Jack is a sweet guy. He reminds me a lot of Ryan in that way.

> **Me:** For Jack, I may be willing to take on a hoard of guys.

"Miss Davis. Please pay attention." I cringe as my teacher calls me out.

I slip the phone into my pocket, about dying when it vibrates again. I can't tell you what was taught the rest of class because I was so focused on what he said.

The moment class is over, I rush out into the hall, pulling my phone out of my pocket.

> **Avi:** Should I be jealous of this newfound friendship with Jack?

I can't help the smile that spreads across my face.
Jealous?

Why does the thought of Xavier being jealous heat my blood?

> **Me:** Don't worry, Avi, You're still my number one boo. *Blowing kiss emoji.*

For the first time in a long time, my chest feels light. I almost feel like the old Cassi. Leaning against the wall, I wait for his text back.

> **Avi:** Good. I'd hate to have to take out a friend for poaching on my territory.

The way he flirts with me brings back those butterflies in my stomach. I know it's just innocent flirting, but I can't help but wonder what it would be like if its real.

> **Me:** Territory? You're such a caveman.
> **Avi:** Damn right. You woman. Me Man. Get in my cave.

I burst out laughing, looking around to make sure no one noticed.

> **Me:** Sure. Right after I club your ass over the head. That's not the way to get a woman.
> **Avi:** Well, wise one. What is the way to get a woman?

My heart stutters. Is he asking how to get me or another woman?
Red hot fury fills my veins at the thought.
Fuck, this is worse than I thought. I shouldn't have slept in his bed last night.
Shoving the phone in my pocket, I make my way out of the building, trying to calm down.
The light feeling from before flees, letting a panic set in. For a moment, I

was actually happy. I was focused on something other than Ryan.

I don't know which caused me more anxiety at the moment. The thought that I could forget Ryan for even a second or that the happiness I had found could be ripped away.

"Cass." I hear in the distance.

I glance back and offer a small smile as Mara jogs over to me.

"Hey, Mara. What's up?"

"What's up with me? No. What's up with you? I haven't seen much of you lately. I thought we were best friends." Her pout isn't lost on me.

This is how Mara is. Everything has to be centered around her. I know it killed her to be out of the spotlight when Ryan died.

Ryan.

"Yeah, I've been going to class and stuff," I murmur, looking around for an escape.

I really am not in the mood for the Mara show.

"Or is it that new hottie you're banging? Jared told everyone about him. The East Coast newbie that came in and swept you off your feet. Stole you right from under Jared's nose."

I scoff. "Seriously? I was never Jared's to begin with. He was a mistake. I'm going to have to have a talk with him."

"You're not denying it, though. Is Xavier your new boyfriend for real? I thought it was fake."

My eyes narrow on hers. "What? Are you jealous? Do you have a thing for him?"

She holds her hands up. "If he's yours, then he's off-limits, but I'd be lying if I said I wasn't interested."

Shaking my head, I turn and walk away,

"What the fuck, Cassi?" Mara grabs my arm, turning me back around.

"You believe Xavier is my boyfriend and you still have the balls to tell me you're interested in him? What kind of friend does that?"

She sneers, "The same friend who sleeps with Jared knowing I had a crush on him throughout high school."

I roll my eyes. "I've apologized to you countless times for that. It's not like I purposely slept with him to hurt you. I honestly don't know why I did it, but I know it was a mistake. Not only because it hurt you, but because it shouldn't have happened."

"Right. Ryan would be so disappointed in you."

I surge forward, but stop when she smirks.

"You know what? Fuck you. Don't bother calling me anymore. I'm tired of your petty shit."

"Fine. Be that way," she calls to my back as I walk away from her. "I'll be sure to tell my mother what a whore you are so she can tell yours."

"I'll tell mine what a cunt you are, so we're even," I call back over my shoulder.

I make it back to my room, but my anger hasn't faded. If anything, it's more inflamed.

"Who pissed in your cereal this morning?" Rebecca asks as she puts on a pair of earrings.

"Mara's such a cunt."

Rebecca stops, turning to me, her mouth wide open.

"What?" I snap.

"I'm just surprised. What did Mara do?"

"She's still pissed I slept with Jared. She doesn't care why or that I was messed up then. Not saying that completely excuses my behavior, but that doesn't mean she has the right to openly admit she wants Xavier. Well, she can't have him."

Rebecca's smile flames the blood boiling beneath my skin. "You think this is funny?"

"No. Not at all. I'm proud of you. You're finally seeing her true colors."

Some of the anger slips out as she comes over and hugs me.

"Thanks. I guess I always knew she was nasty, but I didn't realize until tonight."

"Well, either way, I'm proud. Don't worry about her interest in Xavier either. That boy is smart enough to avoid a snake and if he isn't Jack sure as hell is."

I take a deep breath, letting it whoosh from my mouth. "Thanks. I shouldn't care if she gets with Xavier, but he deserves better."

She winks at me. "He deserves a good girl like you."

I chuckle. "He deserves better than me."

"Whatever you say. I'm going out. Want to come? Or do you need me to stay in with you?"

"No. You go on. I'm going to decompress."

"'Kay. Let me know if you need me. I'll have my cell on me."

I give her a small smile, falling back on my bed as soon as she shuts the door.

My phone vibrates in my pocket, so I pull it out.

Six texts and one missed call.

I read the texts first.

> **Avi:** Too much?
>
> **Avi:** Adra??

Clicking out of his message, I see the other four messages are from Mara. I ignore her.

Looking at the missed call, I see it's from Xavier. Pressing redial, I put the phone to my ear.

"I'm sorry."

His voice is like a calming balm to my anger.

"Avi, there's no reason to be sorry."

"Really? You kind of dipped out on me."

"It has nothing to do with you. I had a confrontation with Mara on the walk home."

"Oh, I'm sorry. Mara is the chick from the bar, right?"

"Yeah." My body tenses at the fact he remembers her.

"I didn't like that she let you walk out the door with a stranger. I'm sorry that you had an argument with her, though. Want to talk about it?"

The tension leaves me at his words. "You didn't like her?"

"Hell no. I mean, she's not really my type, anyway. Too showy. She seems like she would be twenty-four-seven drama."

I chuckle. "You have her pegged. She sure likes you though."

I bite my lip, waiting for his response.

"She's not really my type."

"What's your type?" I don't miss how my voice sounds huskier.

He hums for a moment before answering. "I'd say I'm attracted to blonde hair, blue eyes, with an ass to die for. Too bad they are always so mouthy."

"Hey, I'm not mouthy," I protest, my heart stuttering in my chest at his words.

"Who said I was talking about you, Adra?"

My stomach drops. "I mean, you said blonde with blue eyes, so I just…" I trail off.

He chuckles. "I'm kidding. You're the only blonde hair blue-eyed girl I talk to. Besides, despite your protest, you are totally mouthy as fuck. Your protest only proves my point."

"I really want to argue, but I feel like that would be digging the hole deeper, so instead, I am going to change the subject."

"Sure, quit before you lose. I get what you're doing. Since we are changing the subject, how about you answer my question."

"What was that?"

"What does it take to get a woman?" His voice drops a couple of octaves. My skin heats.

"Well, it depends on the type of woman. If you're looking for one like Mara, well, you already have it all. All you need to do is crook your finger at her and she'll come."

"No, not like Mara. Someone more my type. More like you."

I feel a little dizzy at how fast my heart is beating. "A good, southern girl?"

He hums, "Mmhmm."

I let out the deep breath I was holding. "We like a little romance. Don't get me wrong. We secretly love a little jealousy. Just a touch of possessiveness showing us you care, but we also want some sweet words and a tender touch. A genuine conversation, proving that we are more than our bodies to you. That you value our mind too."

I can feel the tension through the phone. I feel raw. Exposed. Like I just gave him a hand-drawn map to me.

As if he can sense my panic, he clears his throat.

"Romance, huh? No wonder your single, Adra. Men aren't romantic. That's some pussy shit," he teases.

I let out a short laugh, feeling that panic recede. "A girl can dream, right? I mean, is it too much to ask for a man to surprise a chick once in a while? Maybe some random flowers or a trip somewhere?"

"I think you've been watching too many romance movies. Don't give us men too much credit. We don't think that far ahead."

I let out a playful sigh. "One day, maybe."

"You hold out for it. You deserve only the best."

My fingers reach up on their own to touch my lips as I feel a smile spread across them.

How did I go from a ball of fury to a smiling fool within minutes?

He does that to you.

"Thank you. That means a lot."

"Good." I hear a commotion in the background on his end of the phone. "Fuck, Jack. Chill out, man."

I chuckle. "Tell Jack if he doesn't chill I'll come kick his ass."

He repeats my words, causing Jack to grumble in the background.

"Listen, Jack is drunk as fuck at the moment. I don't know what he was thinking drinking early, but I'm going to take care of him. I'll text you tomorrow?"

I smile to myself. "Text me whenever you want. 'Night Avi."

"'Night Adra."

Hanging up the phone, I stare at the ceiling. I can't help the lightness that fills me every time I talk to him. It's like he's breathing new life into me.

I can't help but feel like if I'm not careful, I could get addicted to this feeling.

CHAPTER FIVE

Cassi

Walking out of my last class for the day, I head off toward my dorm.

"Ace." I spin, smiling as Jack makes his way through people to get to me.

"Noob. How are you doing today?" I ask as he stops in front of me.

"I'm not a noob." He glares, but the hint of a smile throws the look off. "You're just an ace. Anyway, not why I'm here. What are you doing tonight, tomorrow, and well for the entire weekend?"

I narrow my eyes. "Why do I feel like I'm being conned into something?"

His eyes grow wide. "Why Miss Davis, I would never dare to con you the way you conned me. One of us has to be the good influence in this friendship."

I roll my eyes. "I'm free this weekend. Why?"

"Wrong answer. You are busy hanging out with us this weekend. Go home and pack. We're going on an adventure." He skips away from me.

"Wait. Where are we going? What do I need to pack?" I call out after him.

He turns, walking backward, and repeats himself, "An adventure, Ace. Pack for an adventure."

An adventure.

What the hell are these boys getting me into now?

Pulling out my phone, I call Xavier as I hustle to the dorm.

He answers on the first ring.

"You all packed?" His warm voice fills my ear.

"You send your lap dog to do all your errands?" I quip.

His chuckle fills the air, making the butterflies swarm my belly. "Jack was already on campus. I planned to accost you at your dorm, but he wanted to be the one to break it to you."

"Sure. Likely story. Are you even going to give me a hint on where we are going?"

"Nope." He pops the P.

"At least tell me what to wear then."

His voice gets husky. "You want me to pick out outfits for you?"

My breath catches at the heat in his tone. "I want to be dressed appropriately."

He groans, "Fuck, if you let me choose I'd pack the skimpiest clothes I could find." He clears his throat. "Two hints. It will be warm and there will be water. That's all you get."

I smile. "One more question."

"I can't tell you anymore."

"Fine, but can you tell me if my roommate is invited," I ask.

"Sure. We can make room for her."

"Thanks, Avi. I'll be ready in an hour. Pick me up?"

"Of course. Can't have you dragging your millions of suitcases all the way over here."

"Hey, I resent that."

"You forget I know other females. I bet you will have at least two with you."

"What's my prize when I win?"

"You mean if you win? Anything you want. Winner's choice."

"Great. This trip is looking better and better."

"Go pack before I regret this impromptu trip."

"Bye, Avi."

I hang up as soon as I hear his goodbye and call Rebecca.

"What's up? You coming out tonight?" she asks over the loud bass of the music in the background.

"No, but you might want to come home. We've been invited on a trip."

"Really? Where?"

"It's an adventure. You have an hour before they come pick us up. Better hurry home," I tell her, letting myself into our room.

I hang up the phone before she can respond and chuckle when she immediately calls back.

Ignoring her call, I pull out my bags. I can only have one, so I need to choose wisely.

Going to my closet, I sift through my choices.

It's going to be a three-day trip, but you don't count today. So really only two outfits, sleep clothes, and a spare outfit just in case.

I grab a sundress, one pair of jeans, one pair of shorts, and three t-shirts. Grabbing my panties and bras, I remember his second clue. Water. Does that mean the beach? Or a pool?

I grab two bathing suits just in case. Then I grab my toiletries bag, which already has all my hygiene items packed carefully inside.

Looking at my haul, I glance back to my options for bags.

I could win by choosing the biggest one, which would easily fit everything I need, but I want to impress him. He thinks he can paint a broad stroke against all women.

Let's show him.

Picking one of my backpacks up, I pack my clothes inside. It's a tight fit, but I smile with victory in my veins as it zips closed.

"I'm here. Don't leave me," Rebecca busts in the door out of breath.

"Are you okay?" I take her appearance in.

She's sweaty and her face is red. She's resting her hands on her knees as she gasps for air.

"Did you run here?"

"Yes. I couldn't find a ride. Now where the hell are we going and how much longer do I have to pack." She straightens and goes to her closet, still out of breath.

"I have no idea where we are going, but Jack and Xavier are going with us. They planned it, actually. As for your time limit." I glance at my phone. "You have about fifteen minutes left."

She groans. "Fine. Back up. This is going to get ugly."

I sit back on my bed and watch as she pulls out her largest suitcase and starts tossing things inside.

"Do you really need that much?" I ask, but she practically growls at me, so I stay quiet while she packs.

Almost fifteen minutes on the dot, she closes her second duffel bag before sitting on her bed.

"All done," she says on a sigh.

My phone vibrates in my hand.

Avi: Coming up.

"Perfect timing. You were almost left behind," I tease Rebecca.

"Like you could leave me behind. I would've hunted your ass down." She throws her arm around my shoulder just as the boys knock on the door.

"Beautiful ladies. Are you ready to go?" Jack sweeps in the room with Xavier following behind.

"Are those your bags?" He gestures to Rebecca's.

"Nope. This is it." I turn, showing him the backpack on my back.

"Seriously? Could you even fit anything in there?"

I shrug. "Well, the panties wouldn't fit so I'll be going commando for the trip, but I figured you wouldn't mind."

I swear his mouth drops open as Jack howls with laughter behind him.

Rebecca slides in next to me. "Do you mind, Xavier? If my girl here doesn't wear panties the entire trip?"

He swallows hard. "Nope. So what prize do you want?"

I shake my head. "You never said there was a time limit. I'm still deciding what I want."

"By all means, take your time," he says sarcastically.

"I will. Thank you," I say, walking out the door.

I can hear Jack shamelessly flirting with Rebecca, making me smile. He's such a flirt, but if anyone can be a match for him, it's her. She doesn't put up with anyone's shit.

"Shotgun," I call as we make our way to Xavier's car.

"Hey," Rebecca half-heartedly complains.

"Is that your prize?" Xavier teases.

"Nope. Just road trip rules." I shoot him a wink before getting in the car, putting my bag at my feet.

As Jack helps Rebecca with her bags, Xavier joins me in the car. "Who said we were going on a road trip?"

"Well, if it requires an overnight stay, I would have to say it's quite a bit away."

"Clever girl. I'll have to watch out for you," he says as he turns on the car.

Jack and Rebecca get into the back seat, bickering already.

"All right, kids. Settle down." Xavier smiles over at me.

"Can you tell me where we are going now?" Rebecca asks.

"Nope." Xavier looks at her in his rearview mirror. "It's a surprise."

As he pulls the car on the road, I hear Rebecca mumble to herself, "If that ain't the most serial killer thing I've ever heard."

I chuckle as Jack tries to draw her into conversation. I reach over and turn on the radio, putting it on my favorite country station.

"Driver picks the music," Xavier says, reaching to turn the station.

I swat his hand. "Passenger is DJ. Road trip law. Everyone knows this."

"So I have eight hours of country to look forward to?"

My eyes widen at the little tidbit he let slip. "Eight hours? Are we going to Corpus Christi?"

He smirks. "Maybe. Or maybe we are going to Oklahoma."

I pretend to shudder. "Don't even joke. Okies hate us Texans."

"Do they really?"

I shrug. "Everything is bigger in Texas. Especially our egos."

He shakes his head, laughing. "You're something else."

I feel a smile creep onto my face. "I sure am. My daddy always told me so."

About two hours into the road trip, I turn down the music.

"Hey, I like that song," Rebecca mumbles from the back seat.

"I know, it's a classic."

"I can't take my eyes off of you," we sing at the same time.

"Girls are weird." Jack mumbles.

"It's from a classic!" I protest.

"I don't know it." Xavier laughs.

"You've never watched *10 Things I Hate About You*?" I ask.

"No, why should I have?"

"It's a classic," Rebecca says from the back.

"If you say so. It sounds like a chick flick." Jack smirks.

"Anyway, I think we should play a game."

"A game?" Avi asks.

"What game?" Jack says.

"Start with the license plate game?" I ask, looking at Xavier, then Jack and Rebecca in the backseat.

"Sounds good to me." Xavier smiles.

"You're going down this time, Davis," Jack says, cracking his knuckles, making us laugh.

"This is going to be good." Rebecca smirks.

I turn back around, leaning forward.

"What are you doing?" Xavier asks, laughter in his voice.

"I'm getting closer," I deadpan, making him laugh.

"Pretty sure you leaning forward won't help you out at all." He reaches over, tapping my knee. "Alabama." He nods toward the car in front of us.

"What no way! How can you read that?" I say as we approach a car that does in fact have an Alabama plate.

"I was blessed with good eyesight," he says, rubbing his lip, trying to cover his smile.

I turn around in time and catch another car's plate. "California." I point at the car.

Jack groans from the back seat. "You guys can see everything before we do."

"Maybe if you spent more time looking out the window, then at me you would have better luck," Rebecca teases, making Xavier and I laugh.

"Idaho!" Jack calls out, ignoring her comment.

For the next hour we go back and forth calling out different states.

"Is it just me or would we have better luck calling out religious signs then finding the random non-Texas driver?" Xavier asks, tapping away at the steering wheel.

"Welcome to the Bible belt," I quip as he pulls off the interstate to get gas.

"Thank god, I need to pee." Rebecca sighs.

"You could have spoken up sooner and I would have stopped," Xavier tells her as he puts the car in park at a gas pump.

"All good, city boy. I would have spoken up at some point," she says before jumping out of the car. "Come on!" she yells at me.

I grab my purse and get out and follow her in. After doing our business and loading up on snacks, we get back on the road. I don't know if it's the people I'm with, but this is the best road trip I've ever been on.

"Cassi, wake up. We're here." I feel a gentle shake on my arm.

I don't know when I fell asleep, but it always happens. There is something about being in a car that calms me to the point where I need to sleep.

Maybe my mom drove around a lot in the car with me when I was a baby.

"Where are we?" I groan and stretch.

"Open your beautiful eyes and look."

I open my eyes and look around. It's dark, but even in the dark, I can tell we are at the gulf. I smile big.

"Do I get another prize for guessing where we were going?"

He chuckles. "I kinda ruined the surprise, huh?"

"Not at all. I love the beach. Thank you for inviting me."

He smiles warmly and whispers, "Anytime."

"You two going to sit in the car all night?" Jack hollers from the door of a beautiful beach house.

"Whose house is this?" I ask as I climb out of the car.

"Jack's parents own it. It's their beach house. When he suggested we make a weekend trip, I thought you might want to join us."

"Aww, you couldn't picture spending a weekend without me, Avi?"

He shakes his head. "There's that Texas-size ego, huh?"

I grab my bag, moving past him toward the house. I marvel at how beautiful it is.

The house is up on stilts with parking beneath. As I make my way up the stairs, I smile as I see the porch swing on the deck. I make my way over to the railing and look out over the dark ocean. Taking a deep breath, I savor the smell of fresh salt air.

Closing my eyes, I listen as the waves crash upon the shore.

"I love it," I say as I feel Xavier come up beside me.

"I'm glad. I wasn't sure if the beach was your thing."

"How could it not be? Listen to the waves. Isn't it the most calming thing you've ever heard?"

He's silent for a moment. "I guess it is. I've never thought about it that way."

"Cassi, this place is gorgeous. Come check out your room," Rebecca calls from inside.

I smile at Xavier as I pass him, making my way into the house. The inside is as gorgeous as the outside.

There's tile flooring throughout with warm beach colors painted on the walls. There are photos of Jack and his family lining the walls, but there are also paintings of the beach itself. I peek into the kitchen, smiling at the granite countertops and the hand towels embroidered with the words "Life's A Beach."

If I had a beach house, it would look exactly like this. I yawn again.

"Come on, you can look around in the morning. Let's head to bed," Xavier says, ushering me upstairs.

He stops and points to a door to my right. "That's yours."

"Which room is yours?"

"This one," he says, walking backward into the room across from mine.

Interesting.

"Goodnight, Adra." He smiles.

"'Night, Avi," I say, shutting the door softly.

Temptation across the hall, however, will I resist?

Xavier

I SLIDE A plate of bacon onto the counter in front of Jack just as the girls come down the stairs.

"Be still my beating heart!" Rebecca proclaims. "Not only is he hot, but he can cook!" she teases.

"I'm more than a pretty face," I deadpan, making everyone laugh.

Rebecca sits next to Jack while Cassi moves toward the fridge. She takes a bottle of water out and drinks half of it in one go.

"Thirsty?"

"Yeah, I didn't drink enough water yesterday," she says as she sets the bottle down on the counter. "This looks good, you make everything?" she asks as she looks at the food.

"All but the cinnamon rolls. Jack popped those in the oven," I tell her, leaning against the counter.

"I'm impressed."

"Don't be," I tell her, popping a piece of bacon in my mouth. "The rolls came from a can. Hardly any work."

She leans against the counter, mimicking me, taking a bite of bacon and all. "Still impressed."

"I aim to please." I smirk, making her blush. "You sleep okay?"

"I did. What about you?"

"Can't complain."

"Jesus, the sexual tension between them is so thick you could cut it with a knife," Rebecca mumbles shoving food into her mouth, making Jack choke on his food.

Cassi blushes again. Clearing my throat, I straighten, taking the attention off of her.

"So, what's the plan for today?" I ask everyone.

Cassi shoots me a grateful look.

"I plan on sitting my ass in a chair in my little bikini and not moving until the sun goes down," Rebecca says.

"Beach day all day, then tonight bonfire."

"On the beach?" Rebecca asks.

"On the beach," Jack agrees. "I can make a few calls and see if any of the people I usually hang out with are around or it could just be the four of us. What do you think?"

"Sounds like a plan, big man," Rebecca says.

"Sounds good to me," Cassi and I say in unison.

"Let's get changed and get out there," Jack says, slapping the counter.

Slowly, I follow the girls up the stairs and watch them break off into their room. I head into the en suite attached to my room and turn on the shower.

God, I thought Cassi was gorgeous before, but seeing her first thing in the morning? She takes my breath away. Stepping into the shower, I hiss as the water pounds onto my back.

What is she doing in her room? Is she taking a shower? Is she thinking of me?

Groaning, I fist my cock, stroking myself. Up and down. Up and down. I picture Cassi in the shower. Head tilted back, hands in her hair, nipples hard as water cascades down her body. I bite my lip as I stroke myself harder, faster. She steps closer, her breasts brushing against my chest as she drops to her knees. I swear I can feel her hands on me. Right as she takes me into her mouth, I explode, shooting my release all over my hand as the water rains down on me. Breathing hard, I lean against the wall.

Let's hope if she ever puts her mouth on me, I don't blow that fast.

"Come on, let's go!" Jack bangs on the bathroom door.

I hang my head. "Give me a minute!" I yell back as I reach for the body wash. Rushing through the shower, I get out and come to a stop when I see Jack lounging on my bed.

"What are you doing?"

"Take you long enough?" he grouches.

Ignoring him, I walk over to my bag and grab my trunks. I slip them on under my towel. Turning toward Jack, I run the towel back through my hair.

"Are they ready?"

"Yeah, I heard them head downstairs."

Tossing the towel onto the bathroom counter. "Then let's go."

Jack jumps off the bed and pushes me out of his way. "Ha! Beat you!"

"What are we six?"

"You ready?" Cassi says as we round the corner into the kitchen, stopping me dead in my tracks as she turns around.

She's wearing a black bikini. The top looks like a spaghetti strap tank top that ends right below her breasts, dipping down, showing her cleavage. The bottoms are high-waisted boy shorts that go up to her belly button, covering all the fun parts.

Cassi bends down, picking up a piece of cinnamon roll that fell onto the floor.

Or maybe not, I think as I see the bottom of her butt cheeks peek out.

Jack elbows me in the side, making me grunt. "You're drooling," he whispers under his breath.

I look over at him and he basically has hearts jumping out of his eyes the way he's looking at Rebecca.

"Like you're so much better," I mumble.

"You guys good?" Cassi asks, tilting her head.

"We're good," I tell her, walking toward the back door.

The girls pass by mumbling a thank you.

"I got the chairs!" Jack tells them as he walks past me. I shut the door and concentrate on breathing.

I just got off, and she has me hard all over again.

It's going to be a long day.

❦

THE GIRLS LAY on the beach most of the day while Jack and I go between messing around in the ocean and tossing the football back and forth.

"Hey, you guys hungry?" Rebecca calls from her chair.

"What do you have in mind?" Jack yells back.

"I don't know, how about you come help me figure that out?" she teases, making him groan.

"God, she's beautiful," he whispers.

"I thought you weren't ready for the take-home type of girl," I quip.

"Hell, as far as I know, she could be both." He winks, running up the beach. He picks Rebecca up out of her chair, making her squeal as he carries her toward the house.

I turn back to the water, wading in slowly. Next thing I know, something hard hits my back, making me fall forward. I hear Cassi squeak right as I go under. While underwater, I move her from my back to my front as I stand back up.

"Really?" I deadpan as I walk us deeper into the water.

"I couldn't help myself." She shrugs as she wraps her legs around my waist.

Thank god the water is cold enough to stop me from rising to the occasion.

"How's your day been?" I ask, trying to push away my wayward thoughts.

"I can't complain."

I run the pad of my thumb along her cheekbone. "You got a little sun."

"The curse of being a blonde."

I step back, stepping on something hard and begin to go down but catch us just in time. Cassi gasps as she falls into me, breasts pushing against my chest, lips ghosting mine.

"Hey love birds, you coming?" Jack yells from the house, making Cassi jerk back. I walk forward and as soon as we're out of the water, I set her down.

She clears her throat. "Well, that was fun."

"Yeah," I say, watching her walk away. I adjust my aching cock as I follow behind.

Walking into the kitchen, I see Rebecca and Jack set out chips and sandwich stuff.

"This looks good," Cassi tells them as she grabs what she wants.

"I figured this would be easiest for now and then later order some pizza before we have a bonfire." Jack shrugs.

"Makes sense." I nod as I grab a plate, helping myself.

The three of them fall into easy conversation while I eat in peace. My phone rings on the counter.

Finley.

"Hey, I have to take this," I tell them as I grab my phone.

"Hello?" I answer as I walk up the stairs.

"Hey man, how are you?" Fin asks.

"I'm good? Everything okay?"

"What a guy can't call another guy for the hell of it?" he jokes.

"Sure, you can call one of the Yates or even Sterling. Last I checked, we weren't close enough to be phone buddies," I say honestly as I shut the bedroom door.

"Yeah, I guess you're right." He sighs. "Look, I have a favor."

"Okay, name it," I tell him as I lean against the window frame, staring at the waves.

"You know I was into some shit last year," he breaks off, gathering his thoughts. "I was wondering how you would feel about Tins coming and visiting sometime."

"She's always welcome." I frown. "That bad?"

"Nah, everything's good. But I know if she was here while I do what I need to do, all she will do is worry."

"She likes to worry." I laugh. "Look, you know she's always welcome to visit. We're good."

"As long as you know she's mine," he jokes, lightening the mood, making us both laugh.

"Yeah, you have nothing to worry about there."

"Oh, does Xavier have a girlfriend?" he sing-songs.

"We're not having this conversation Fin."

"Oh, come on, give me something!"

"Goodbye, Fin." I laugh as I hang up.

I leave the room, walking down the stairs, making my way back outside.

"Hey, where are the girls?" I ask Jack.

"They wanted to hit the shops down the street." He shrugs, eyes closed as he chills in a deck chair.

"Ah." I nod.

"Everything okay?"

"Yeah, why?"

"You were frowning when you saw who was calling you."

"Nah, it was Fin. We're not exactly friends, so it was a little random. Everything is good though."

"Good." Jack nods. "So, you and Ace looked pretty cozy in the water." He teases, making me laugh.

"It's nothing."

"Whatever helps you sleep at night." He shrugs. "Just make sure you cover her face with a pillow when you fuck her." He shivers. "I really don't want to hear her moaning," he says making me laugh.

CHAPTER SIX

Cassi

I flick between the hangers on the rack, checking out different graphic t-shirts.

"So," Rebecca drawls, peeking between the clothes and myself.

"Spit it out," she says, making me sigh.

"What do you want me to say?"

"I want you to tell me you're into Xavier and won't go back to dipshit."

"I was never with Jared."

"Might as well have been with the way he acts," she scoffs. "Look, I just want you to be happy and healthy. Jared doesn't make you happy and is toxic."

"You just don't understand our relationship."

"See, that's where you're wrong," she says, giving up on looking at the clothes. "I grew up with those guys too. I know your dynamic. You and Jared only hooked up out of grief. And Xavier? He could bring you back to the land of living. He could help you move on."

"He makes me smile," I mumble.

"See!"

"Mara put the moves on him and he turned her down." I smile, thinking about when he met her at the bar.

"Fuck Mara," Rebecca spits out.

"Rebecca," I sigh.

"No, seriously, I'm so glad you finally saw her for who she really is. Between her and Jared, I don't know who's worse for you," she says, angrily searching the clothing rack again.

"You know, I don't like walking away from people. Especially now."

"Because your loyalty knows no bounds. You can't keep holding onto the old because of sentimentality. It's okay to remember the good times fondly, but you don't need to keep giving them your everything when all they do is take." She sighs. "Look, why don't you just give whatever it is between you and Xavier a chance. It doesn't have to be forever but, I think it could be if you guys give it a chance."

She's my best friend, but I haven't told her I've already been feeling that way. Our texts are daily. Our phone calls almost as frequent. When we aren't calling or texting, it's usually because we are hanging out together. Sometimes it's alone, while other times it's with Jack and some other guys.

"I'll think about it okay?" I tell her. "Now, what do you think of this?"

"I think it will make Xavier lose his mind and you should wear it tonight." She deviously smirks.

I look down at the dark green lace bralette that ties between the breasts. Typically, it's something I would never wear but when at the beach.

"Pair it with a pair of white shorts," Rebecca encourages.

"I do have a pair," I murmur, thinking about how the top would look with the shorts.

Would Xavier like it? Only one way to find out.

"Fuck it," I say breathlessly as I hang the hanger over my arm.

"That's my girl!" Rebecca cheers. "Now let's check out and get ready for tonight," she says as she walks toward me. Rebecca grabs my wrist and pulls me toward the registers, making me laugh.

"Slow down."

"No time to waste! We have prepping to do."

The five-minute walk to the shops seems to take much less time as Rebecca continues to power walk back to the house. I'm nearly out of breath just trying to keep up with her.

Once back at the house, Rebecca ushers me upstairs to get ready. I take a quick shower, washing the grime away and blow dry my hair. As I step out of the shower, I find Rebecca sitting on the counter, feet in the sink, applying her makeup.

"You're ridiculous." I shake my head as I dry off.

"You know it." She winks as I throw my hair up in the towel.

Hustling into my room for the weekend, I get dressed in the green top and white shorts. Walking back into the bathroom, I come to a stop.

Damn, I look good.

Even with no makeup and a towel on my head.

"He's going to swallow his tongue," Rebecca says gleefully as I grab her blow dryer.

"Whatever you say," I tell her as I plug it in.

Twenty minutes later my thick hair is dry and large and in charge.

"Can I curl it?" Rebecca asks as I wrap the blow dryer up.

"If you brought your curling wand." I shrug as I reach for my makeup. After quickly putting on the basics and her doing my hair, we head downstairs, finding the guys once again in the kitchen, music on and pizza on the counter.

Jack whistles. "Damn. I don't know about you X, but I'm feeling pretty lucky tonight," he boasts.

"Jack," Xavier warns, never looking away from me.

I bite my lip, looking away. "So, what kind of pizza did you get?"

"Ham, right?" Xavier clears his throat, pushing a box toward me.

"Thanks." I smile at him as I take a piece from the box.

Xavier and I eat in silence as Rebecca and Jack talk enough for the both of us.

"We should probably start the fire," Xavier says, abruptly.

"I'm game," Jack says, tossing his paper plate in the trash.

I watch as Xavier takes his time, wiping his hands off on a napkin and wiping off the counter under his plate before he tosses his trash.

"Meet you out there," he says to me as he passes.

"Sounds good," I whisper.

As soon as the back door closes Rebecca cackles.

"What's so funny?" I frown.

"Oh, god, the sexual tension! I swore the room was going to light on fire with the way you two looked at each other!"

"Shut up," I mumble.

"You want to take a ride on his disco stick," she sings, making me laugh.

Well, she's not wrong.

"Keep it down. They could come in at any minute."

Her eyes widen. "So you're admitting it?"

I roll my eyes at her while I busy myself putting the leftovers away.

"I'll admit that I find him very attractive, but he's a friend. A very good friend. I don't know if I want to ruin that."

She slides up next to me, wrapping her arm around my shoulder. "My mom always says that relationships are built on trust and a strong friendship. Looks like you got that down. Why not give it a shot?"

"I'm scared," I admit softly.

"Of what?" she asks just as gently.

"I haven't told anyone, but Xavier makes me feel alive. Like he has awoken a part of me that has been paralyzed since Ryan died. What happens if I act on these feelings I'm having and it ruins our friendship? What if I'm just now getting back to normal and one wrong step derails all of my progress?"

She gives me a tight smile. "I can't answer those questions for you. All I can tell you to do is follow your heart. You can't be afraid of living your life because you might lose someone. If you do, then before you know it your life will pass you by and leave you with nothing to show for it. What if you pass on this and in ten years, you find out he's married with kids and you look back and wonder what it would have been like if you had taken that chance? Would you be able to live with the 'what-ifs?'"

My heart stops at the thought of him with someone else. I don't know exactly when it happened, but she's right. My feelings for him have been growing and changing since day one. I might have planned to stay just friends, but I'm not sure that's even a possibility anymore. Can I continue on the way we are going? What happens if he gets a girlfriend? I don't think I could stand around and watch him flirt with another woman the way he does with me.

"You're right. Tonight, I lay my cards on the table and see where his head is at."

"Well, I can tell you where his eyes were at. On you throughout dinner. He couldn't stop watching you."

"Stop it." I smack her arm.

She grabs my hand, holding it. "Babe, I know you've had it rough, but you have to start living your life. I'm not saying forget about what happened or don't feel your pain. I don't think that pain will ever go away fully, but this man makes you smile. I mean, I haven't seen you brighten up the way you do with him with anyone else, even before everything. So all I'm saying is consider it."

I let out a deep sigh. "Okay. I'll think about it."

She wraps her arm in mine. "Great. Let's get out there. I see others filtering up."

I let her pull me out on the back deck and down the stairs. I can see Jack and Xavier by a small fire in the distance. Standing right next to them? Two beautiful girls.

A pang in my chest hits me.

I wish Rebecca had kept her big mouth shut. I don't want to confront my feelings for this man. Especially if it may lead to rejection.

My steps falter as I walk closer, watching as the brunette places her hand on his arm.

I can see her mouth moving and all I can feel is disappointment. She's gorgeous. Of course, he's going to want to spend time with her tonight.

He moves slightly, dislodging her hand before looking back toward the house.

His eyes find mine.

Then he smiles before walking toward me. He wraps his arm around my shoulders, pressing a kiss to the side of my head.

"What…" I start.

"Hey, babe. Come meet, Lindsey. She was just telling me how she loves to dance. I told her you do too," he shouts as he leads me over to the girl.

She sneers at me. "Who is this?"

"This is my girlfriend, Cassandra, who I was telling you about."

My eyes widen slightly, but I try to hide it.

"Oh," the girl huffs. "I think I see my friend waving for me."

She doesn't bother saying goodbye as she hustles over to a group of girls that have gathered a little farther down the beach.

Xavier doesn't let me go once she leaves. Instead, he looks down at me with an amused look on his face.

"What was that?" I ask.

He chuckles. "I'm just following your amazing example. Isn't that how we met? You wanted to get rid of a pushy guy, so you pretended I was your boyfriend?"

I grimace. "I guess so."

"So I figured turnabout's fair play. Now you get to be my girlfriend for the night. Let me tell you, Adra. I expect my girlfriend to be doting."

I roll my eyes at him. "Don't you want to leave yourself open in case you meet a girl you do like? If I pretend to be your girlfriend, I expect respect. No cheating on me, fake or otherwise."

He leans in closer, ghosting his lips across my cheek. "Don't worry. I have no interest in those girls."

I swallow hard. "Well then, I guess I can be your girlfriend for a little while."

"Good. Let's go see what Jack's doing."

He pulls me over to Jack and Rebecca, who are surrounded by a group of people. Xavier never once let go of me, keeping his arm firmly around my shoulder.

I don't miss the way his thumb caresses my shoulder or how he turns, pressing his lips to my temple as he laughs.

This is comfortable.

Maybe Rebecca is right.

Xavier

I sit in a chair in front of the fire, watching the girls dance to the music playing from the portable speaker. I take a sip of my beer and relax back into my chair. Jack's sitting next to me, but he's talking to his friends. Not that I mind. I'm not sure I could concentrate on their conversation, anyway.

No, instead I'm concentrating on one thing.

Her.

I can't seem to get her off of my mind today. I mean, I'm attracted to her obviously, but seeing her today was eye-opening. It wasn't that she looked gorgeous. She always does.

No. The problem was, as soon as I saw her, this possessive feeling rose up inside me. It made me want to drag her into the other room to keep any other set of eyes from laying their eyes on her sun-kissed flesh.

It was the way my body reacted, wanting to reach out and pull her to me. To stake my claim.

I guess that's why I did it. Why I told that girl I was taken.

She didn't care at first, telling me she could keep a secret.

That was, until I introduced her to Cassi, purposely using her God-given name as I know she doesn't like strangers using her nickname.

It was the best move I could have made. It kept Cassi plastered to my side most of the day, which of course kept wandering eyes from lingering too long. Most of the guys here have enough respect for Jack to avoid conflict with his college buddy.

Thank God for small miracles because I don't know what I would do if someone approached her.

I have no right to do anything, really. It's not like we're actually dating. It's a charade meant to keep the women at bay.

At least, that's what I'm telling myself.

I'm not quite ready to explore the real reason I want her to stay close to me.

Cassi glances my way before she says something to Rebecca. Then she saunters over to me. I can't help but smile at her giggle as she drops into my lap. She takes the beer I've been nursing for the past hour and sets it down.

"I was drinking that." I rasp.

Loving the way she feels in my lap as I wrap my hand around her waist. Holding her in place.

These little touches have been coming more frequently lately. A hand hold here. A kiss on the cheek there. I don't know when she became comfortable enough to sit in my lap, but fuck if I don't love it.

Maybe it's the fake relationship thing, or maybe it's the vibe in the air. Whatever it is, I'm thanking my lucky stars right about now.

Cassi snuggles into my side before responding. "Not anymore."

"You having fun?"

"Of course," she says, running her hand down my chest.

"That's some outfit," I tell her, trying not to stare at her breasts that are on display.

I've been trying to keep my eyes off her all night, but I've failed completely.

"You like it?" she says coyly.

"You know I do," I growl, squeezing her tight, making her gasp. "I think every guy who sees you in this would love it."

She smiles brightly. "Take a walk with me?"

I nod as she gets up, easily slipping her hand in mine to help me stand.

We walk down the beach away from our impromptu party in silence.

"Here's good." She pulls on my hand, stopping me.

I drop down into the sand, patting next to me for her to join me.

She doesn't though. Instead, she pushes my knees down before straddling my lap.

My hands immediately come up to her hips, holding her in place. I'm not the only one who noticed this new position. My dick hardens in my pants at the feel of her heat on top of me.

"What are you doing?" I smile at her.

"Shhh. No talkey," she whispers.

I'm about to ask her what she means when she leans in, ghosting her lips over mine as if she's teasing me.

I hesitate for a moment.

"Adra." I smile when I see her shiver. "What are you doing?" I ask again.

"Avi, aren't you tired of all the tension between us?" she whispers before placing a kiss on my cheek.

"If I didn't know any better, I'd think you're drunk," I tell her.

She leans back, but stays in my lap. "I need to tell you something."

"Anything," I tell her, reaching up to brush a stray strand of hair out of her face.

"I like you. I don't know when it happened, but I really like you."

I let out a sigh. "I like you too, Adra, but I'm not sure either of us are really in the right frame of mind to start anything now."

Her bright turquoise eyes peek up at me from under her eyelashes. Tempting me to take back what I said and take her to bed to worship her the way she deserves.

Almost.

Cassi's gorgeous. There's no doubt about that. She's funny and quirky. It's easy to be around her. That's not the problem.

The problem is that she has unresolved issues in her life and I can't put myself through that again. As much as I love Tinsley and am happy for her, I won't put myself in the position to be anyone's second choice. Not again.

The worst part is, the way I've been feeling about Cassi is way more intense than I ever felt about Tinsley. With Tinsley, my ego was wounded, but with Cassi, I don't think I'd leave with my heart intact.

She frowns. "I'm not asking you to marry me."

"What are you asking for then?"

"Friends." She brushes her lips across mine once more. "Friends that are exploring the possibility that there could be something more here? Who's to say friends can't kiss?"

Fuck.

This woman is going to be the death of me.

When I don't respond right away, her face falls. She goes to pull back from me, but I don't let her go.

Fuck it.

I told her I wasn't in a good place and I know she's not either, but she still wants this. As much as I want to, I can't deny her. Maybe I can keep her at a distance while fucking her out of my system. Seems like the perfect combination.

Yeah, right, my brain tells me.

"Are you sure?" I ask, threading one hand into her hair and wrap the other around her waist, pulling her into me, making me gasp.

"What I'm sure of is I can't take it anymore. I want to know what your lips feel like against mine."

I slam my lips down onto hers, taking her into a brutal kiss. Neither one of us is gentle as we press closer, attempting to meld together as one. I swipe my tongue against her lips, urging her to open up. When she doesn't right away, I nip her bottom lip, making her gasp. Taking the moment of surprise,

I slip my tongue into her mouth, rubbing against hers. She doesn't hesitate, moving her tongue into my mouth for its own exploration.

We kiss and kiss for who knows. Hands roving. Her hands make their way under my shirt, up my abs, and around to my back. She grinds down onto me, making me groan.

"Avi," she whimpers.

"Not here, Adra. I won't have our first time be on a beach where sand can get into places it doesn't belong," I tell her, making her laugh.

"I'm sorry," she says once she calms down, pulling back.

"What are you sorry for?"

"Pushing." She sighs, brushing her loose girls away from her face.

"Hey, I like you pushing, but not here. I'm thinking about the both of us when I say no," I tell her, running my thumb over her bottom lip.

"Make-out buddies?"

"For now," I say, making us both smile.

"For now."

CHAPTER SEVEN

Cassi

Avi: What are you wearing right now?

I smile as I peek at the text. I'm starting to regret taking evening classes. It seemed like a great idea. Take all my classes between noon and seven and still have time for a party if I want. Plus, sleeping in is a must. I'm not a morning person.

You know who is a morning person? Xavier Walsh. Meaning while I'm getting my beauty sleep, he's studying hard in class. Then when he's done for the day and wants to see me, I'm in class. Instead of going to a party, we usually meet up for an hour or two before he heads back to his dorm to get some sleep.

Lather, rinse, repeat.

We haven't done anything further than kissing so far, but I want to. I want to bad.

A little voice in the back of my head is telling me to pump the breaks. That part of me is clinging to Xavier for a not so noble reason, but I hush it.

Truth is, I like the way he makes me feel.

He makes me feel like I'm gorgeous. Like my broken pieces aren't a deterrent. It doesn't make me less. Like they just make me well me.

He's a great friend.

My phone buzzes in my hand again. I glance down.

> **Avi:** Ignoring me again? I might have to spank that ass later.

My skin heats as tingles soar down to my core. He's such a damn tease.

If women are cock teases, what do you call men that tease?

A poon-tease? Cunt-tease? Clit-tease?

Whatever it is, Xavier has it on lock.

For the past week, we've been hanging out like friends do. A couple of the guys have been there with us, but sometimes it's just us. Those are the nights I like the most. While the guys are fun to hang out with, Xavier keeps his distance when they're around.

When they aren't though, we end up making out like teenagers. Sometimes his hands roam my body, but they stay away from anything too private. It makes me wonder if he's a virgin.

Would that matter?

Absolutely. Not because I wouldn't still want him, but because I'm a mess myself. I don't really know if men view their virginity like women, but I don't think I could take the responsibility of taking it from someone.

Especially someone I care about.

While we are messing around a little, I still care about Xavier. He's a really good guy. I can tell by the way he's considerate toward the guys or the way he's always doing small things for Jack, when he doesn't realize it. Like buying extra pepper jack cheese to put in the fridge because it's Jack's favorite, even though he doesn't care for it.

Honestly, I'm blown away by Xavier. He may look like your typical rich boy, wearing hundred-dollar shirts and driving an expensive car, but inside, he's down to Earth. He never tries to flaunt his money.

The way he's kind to everyone reminds me of my granddaddy. He was always kind to everyone too. Quick to give a smile or hold open a door for someone, male or female. I find the same in Xavier. If he walks with me to class, he grabs the door. If we go somewhere in his car, he makes me wait for him to open the car door. When we all went to dinner last night, he even quietly paid for an elderly couple's meal who sat next to us. He didn't say anything, but I saw him arrange it with the server. The wink he sent me when he caught me looking melted my panties.

They say all the good men are hard to find. If that's the truth, I know I should be chomping at the bit to claim him, but he has his issues and I have mine.

I smile as my phone buzzes a third time.

Jared: Can we meet tonight?

My stomach drops. It's not Xavier, but Jared. Jared, who I have pushed out of my mind.

I feel guilty for cutting him off, but being around him makes me feel like I'm suffocating.

I know I'm going to need to face him, eventually. He was a huge part of my life and while I've found a way to cope with my grief; I know he has not.

Maybe today's not that day. I tell myself.

Still, as my finger hovers over the "N," I hesitate.

Taking a deep breath, I tell him "yes" instead. Then I let Xavier know I can't meet tonight.

Fuck. Why am I so fucked up?

I don't listen to anything for the rest of class. Not that I was listening in the first place, but at least with Xavier, I was smiling.

Not anymore.

As soon as the teacher lets class out, I head over to the frat house. I don't want to go there, especially with a party going on, but the last time I had him meet me in a public place, we ended up arguing so loud that everyone was staring at us.

That one got back to my dad. I didn't want that call again.

Thankfully, when I arrive at the house, the party isn't in full swing. I give a small smile to a couple of the guys as I make my way up to Jared's room. He said he would wait for me there.

I go to knock on the door, but as I do, it opens a little. I hear a noise, figuring it's Jared getting up, so I wait. When he doesn't come to the door, I open it wider, gasping when I see him.

Jared's ass is facing me as he rams into some unknown person beneath him. By the sounds that are coming out of its mouth, I would say it's a banshee.

"What the fuck?" I yell, pissed that I canceled my standing date with Xavier for this asshole.

He looks over his shoulder and has the audacity to grin. He actually grins.

"Oh, hey, babe. Want to join in?" he asks.

"Fuck you, Jared. Lose my goddamn number."

I slam the door, running down the stairs. I barely take a step toward the door, when a large body runs into me.

"Whoa, slow down. What's wrong?"

I let out a relieved sigh when I realize it's Jack. Then I'm angry again because I'm crying. Not because I'm sad. No, I'm crying because I'm beyond pissed.

"I'm fine. I need to get out of here." I go to walk around him, but he grabs my arm, walking out the front door with me.

"Listen, I can't drive you, but I can wait with you until your ride gets here."

"What? No, I walked."

He laughs. "You think I watched you walk in and didn't tell my boy you were here? X will be here in a minute."

As if he summoned him, Xavier pulls up in front of us. He leaves the car running before jumping out and coming over to me.

"What's wrong? What did that asshole do?"

I look over to Jack with a questioning look.

He shrugs. "We all saw Jared take Mara upstairs. Not long after you walked in heading up there too. I did the math."

My heart clenches.

Mara? I shouldn't be surprised, but somehow I still am. Even though we had a falling out, I didn't think she would do something so cruel. Before I realized it was her, I thought it was just Jared being an asshole, but now? I know she has a part in this.

I let out a sigh. "I'm fine."

Both men ignore me.

"I'm taking her home. Call me if you need a DD," Xavier says to Jack.

He salutes before giving me a sad smile. Xavier opens the passenger door, ushering me inside.

Once we are on the road, I look over at him.

"I don't want to go to the dorm," I whisper.

"Where do you want to go?"

I shrug. "How far are you willing to go?"

"For you? The distance." He winks, making me chuckle.

This is why I like him so much. He seems to know exactly what I need.

"That's cheesy. I want to show you something, but it's about a thirty-minute drive." I look down at my hands in my lap.

He reaches over, grabbing one. "Tell me where to go and we will go."

Why does my hand in his feel so right?

Xavier

WE'VE BEEN QUIET the entire drive except when Cassi gives me directions. It's not long before we pull up to an empty parking lot. It's dark, no street lights here since the parking lot is gravel.

It looks like they are still developing it. Building some type of outdoor park.

"Come on," Cassi whispers, getting out before I can question her.

I get out and rush to her side. "I can't be the prince if you open your own door."

She rolls her eyes, hooking her arm in mine. She leads me down a path until we are surrounded by trees. After several minutes of walking, we come to a lake. I look over at Cassi, smiling as the moon reflects off her skin.

Fuck, she's gorgeous.

Then I notice the tears flowing again.

I fight the urge to pull her into my embrace. I want to comfort her, but the other part, my pride, is bristling at the thought she's upset because of another guy.

Don't do this to yourself again. It warns me. I know how this story always turns out. Me, broken-hearted while she's living her best life with her dream guy.

"This is where my brother and I used to go when we needed space. Sometimes we would come together and hang out. Swim, hike, go for a run, but other times, we would come alone. Whenever one of us was upset, the other knew this is where we could be found."

I can hear the agony in her voice as she speaks. As if the words pouring from her mouth are a dagger, repeatedly slicing her skin.

My heart wins the war, pulling her into my side. "Your brother sounds amazing."

She chokes on a sob before she responds, "He was."

I struggle to find the words to say when I realize what she's saying.

He was.

She lost her brother. I want to relate to her. I want to tell her I understand the pain she feels, but I can't. I've never lost anyone so permanently. Hell, the only loss I've ever really felt was losing Tinsley.

Even then, I can still call her. She's still my friend.

She lost someone in a way that you can never come back from.

"I'm sorry," I finally whisper, running my hand through her hair as I hold her to me.

I let her cry until she can't anymore. When she's quieted, she pulls back to look at me. "I wasn't crying earlier because Jared was with some chick. I was crying because he was my brother's best friend. I was clinging to him because he was one of the last pieces of him I had left. When he passed, Jared and I got close because we were both lost."

"You found comfort in each other. There is nothing wrong with that. Grief can take many forms, even in friendship with another," I tell her, comparing it to the only thing I can relate to it.

Isn't that what I've been doing with Cassi this whole time? Pulling her in, but then pushing her away when I think she's getting too close? Kissing her, but never letting her take it further because I'm afraid she will pull back.

"We did. It was a mistake. I told Jared that after the first time. I knew as soon as we were done that I made a mistake, but still, he kept coming back. I feel like he used me in my weak moments to make himself feel better, which only upsets me even more. He was my brother's best friend and I know my brother would have wanted him to look after me, not take advantage of me. I don't think I even realized that was what he was doing until tonight. He used me to get through his own grief, and when I stopped being there for him, he did something cruel to hurt me. So no, I wasn't crying because of him. I was crying for him in a way. That he is so far gone right now that he can't even see the damage he's done. I want to help him pull himself out of the water, but if I try, I'm afraid I'll drown with him."

I press a kiss to the top of her head. "You can't help someone who isn't ready to be helped. If he is really in a bad place, you can't let him drag you down with him. Tell me, Cass, what changed for you. Why do you feel he is drowning, but you're not anymore?"

She sighs, thinking over my words.

"I knew coming here was going to be difficult for me. Jared and Ryan came here together last year. They joined the same frat and shared many of the same classes. I was a year behind them, so I had to wait. When Ryan died, I didn't even want to come here anymore. I wanted to move far away, hiding from the memories. I couldn't go through with it though. Jared convinced me I would feel closer to Ryan here, but I don't. I think it was his way of manipulating me into staying around. Either way, I'm not mad at him for it. While I might not feel closer to Ryan here. Plus, since it's still close to home, I can run out and see my parents when I want to. Not that I've been doing that much lately. So when I started school here, I decided I was going to move on from my grief. Step one was letting Jared go. I didn't want to lose him as a friend, but I couldn't keep falling into the pattern we had. I might have been lost in my head all summer, but just being here was like a fresh start."

I nod. "That's why you came to me at the party. You were trying to stick to your guns."

"Yeah. I was trying to stay strong. I figured if he thought I was taken, he would leave me alone. I was wrong though. He still seeks me out. Hell, he sought me out even more that first week after we met. He stopped after I started spending so much time in your dorm. I thought he had realized that it was really and truly over. That's why when he texted me tonight and asked me to meet him, I went. I wanted to take the time to clear the air between us. I guess he had different ideas."

"I'm sorry. I wish I could make it better for you."

She squeezes me tighter. "You being here makes it better. You have made it better. I said starting school is what changed, and it did, but honestly, it wasn't just that. Jack has been a great friend, making me laugh when I didn't think I could. Then there's you. You make me feel alive again. Like the pain is still there, but that it isn't always the dominating feeling inside. That helps."

I swallow hard. Hearing her say that I am part of the reason she's surviving makes my chest swell with pride. I've been holding back from her, but from the way she's talking, I have no reason to.

I'm so lost in my thoughts that I almost miss what she says next.

"I can barely stand to even come here anymore. It hurts too much. It's tainted," she whispers.

Cassi

"WHY? WHAT HAPPENED?" His voice pulls me out of my downward spiral.

"Back in May, there was an accident. He didn't make it." Changing the subject, I say, "This was our spot. We used to come here all the time. Ryan was my best friend. I could tell him anything. Whenever things got too heavy, this was our spot. We could come here to be alone, but the other would eventually show up. We weren't twins, but we somehow just knew what the other needed. Sometimes we would sit here in silence. Other times he would let me yell and scream at him. Then there were the times he'd let me cry. This place holds so many memories for me, but it's tainted now. Not the same. As much as I love it here, I also kind of hate it."

I never should have slept with Jared. I knew it; he knew it. But sometimes you take comfort in things that you shouldn't know matter how wrong. Now we're left with nothing. We ruined our friendship a little more every time our clothes came off. Trying to find relief from the grief that never came.

"You can still have your memories, Cass. They will always be in here." He steps closer, pressing his hand over my heart.

I smile weakly. "When we were ten, we carved our names into a tree over there. Let's see if you can still see it."

We walk toward the tree. I run my finger over the engraving.

Ryan + Cassi= BFF.

I can still remember the day we carved it. I was thirteen, and he was fourteen. We rode our bikes here to swim.

"Cass, if I could, I would never leave this place."

I glance at Ryan while he floats on his back next to me.

"Why is that?"

"It's peaceful here. It feels like the sun always shines. It always makes my day better when we come here."

"Even when I yell at you?"

He flips in the water, treading next to me. "Especially when you yell at me."

"That sounds dumb, RyRy. You can't find me yelling peaceful."

He smiles. "Maybe not the actual yelling, but when you let all your feelings out, at the end, there is this peaceful look you get on your face. Like you're relieved to get rid of such strong emotions."

"I think we need to have your head checked."

"You don't understand it, but you will someday."

After a few moments of silence, he says, "Come on, Cass. I have an idea."

I remember feeling irritated that he was making me get out, but I followed him anyway.

"It's cold out here. Let's get back in," I urged him.

"No way. Come on, it'll be fun."

He runs to his bike, me trailing behind. He grabs the pocketknife that he got for Christmas and urges me to follow.

"I'm not going to do a blood ritual with you again. It was stupid and did nothing."

"Stop being a spoilsport. Come on."

I walk behind him, watching as he knocks on several trees. Then he stops, pointing at one.

"This one's perfect, right?"

I look up at the tree. It looks like every other tree. His smile has me keeping that to myself.

"Yeah, RyRy. It's perfect."

He takes his knife and starts carving into the tree.

"What are you doing?" I asked him.

"Leaving our mark that way this will be our peaceful place forever."

I watch as he carves both of our names and stops. "What do you think?"

I scrunch up my nose at him. "I think people are going to think we're a couple."

He looks back at it. "Good point. What to do to make it better though."

As he's musing to himself, I grab his knife.

"Hey, be careful."

"Stop being such a big brother."

I lean in, adding an equal sign and the letters BFF.

"There. Now they will think we are best friends."

He slings his arm around my shoulders. "That's because we are."

Tears continue to flow down my face as I remember that day.

"Ryan said this would mark this as our place forever, but forever is subjective, isn't it? You can say that class is taking forever, and it means one thing while also saying you want to live forever, which is another. This is our mark here, but when does forever end? Will this tree still be here after they clear this land in the next couple of months? Will this one tree be the lucky ones that make it, or will it just be another lost memory for a couple of kids that don't matter to the universe?" I say as I run my hand over our names carved into the tree trunk.

"I can't answer that. I can't predict the future, but I can tell you this. When Ryan said this would mark your place forever, he wasn't talking about anything tangible like a tree. He was talking about the memory you were cementing in your mind and heart. He was talking about the feeling you had when he carved your names into that tree. Those feelings will outlast even the most destructive mind diseases. That's what will be left when forever finally comes."

"You sound so sure." I sigh, turning back toward him.

"Because I am. I know without a shadow of a doubt that he loved you. He wouldn't want you holding onto all this grief, letting it overwhelm you."

"And he wouldn't want me falling into bed with his best friend either, huh?" I quip, making us both laugh.

"No, probably not. Or maybe he would. You know him better than me. One thing I know is he would want you to give yourself a break. Don't be so hard on yourself."

A lightness fills me at his words. I don't know if he even realizes what he said.

Don't be so hard on yourself.

He doesn't know what happened. He has no idea the amount of guilt I harbor, but with that one statement, I feel a small portion leave me.

"You're right. He wouldn't want me to be so hard on myself."

He would want me to forgive myself.

Xavier pulls me into him and starts walking back toward the car. "Come on, why don't you stay with me tonight? We can go back to the dorm, order some food and watch a movie or two. How does that sound?"

"That sounds perfect," I tell him as I bury myself into his side, holding him tight.

"Let's go for now. We can always come back."

I smile weakly up at Xavier. "I hope they don't cut down this tree. As much as it hurts me now, I know I'll want to look at it again one day."

"I hope so too."

Xavier

vw at the TV as Cassi sleeps next to me, face buried in my chest, legs intertwined with mine. I knew she had some sort of past with Jared, I just didn't know how much.

I was clinging to him because he was one of the last pieces of him I had left. When he passed, Jared and I got close because we were both lost.

Can I compete with the past?

You couldn't when it came to Tinsley, the devil on my shoulder says.

But Cassi is different, the angel reminds me.

I can't help but think about the devastation that covered her face tonight when she was talking about Ryan. What's it like to be that close to someone, only to lose them? Can I really blame her for trying to hold on to Jared?

Cassi nuzzles her face into my chest. Looking down, I can't help but think about how beautiful she is as I brush a piece of hair off of her face. My phone buzzing catches my attention and I slowly grab it, hoping not to wake her up.

> **Jack:** You guys good?
> **Me:** Yeah, we're good. You need a ride?
> **Jack:** Nah, I'm going home with someone tonight. Just wanted to check and make sure Ace was good. If she wants, she can take my bed tonight.

I look down at a sleeping Cassi and can't help but smirk.

> **Me:** We're good. Keep me updated if you change your mind and come home.
> **Jack:** Will do. Take care of our girl.

I put my phone back on the nightstand, eyes feeling heavy. Pulling Cassi into my chest, I can't help but think about how right this feels.

Yeah, she's worth the risk.

CHAPTER EIGHT

Cassi

"That class is going to kill me," I tell Rebecca as we walk out of algebra.

"Oh, it's not that bad."

"Easy for you to say miss genius," I mumble without any heat.

"I got you. Don't worry," Rebecca says, bumping her shoulder to mine.

"Thank god for smart besties," I joke, making us laugh.

"Cassi!"

We turn, looking over our shoulders, and see Mara rushing to catch up.

"God, I hate her," Rebecca grumbles.

"Rebecca." I widen my eyes at her.

"What? You don't like her anymore either, remember?"

"Be nice," I chastise.

"Yeah, yeah."

"Hey, Mara. What's up?" I ask as she approaches.

"I haven't seen you in a while," Mara says, brushing hair out of her face.

"Yeah, sorry. I've been a little busy."

I hear Rebecca mumbling under her breath.

"Too busy for your best friend?" She raises a brow.

"Yeah, no. She's been spending time with me. Thanks for asking," Rebecca chimes in, arms crossed over her chest.

"Rebecca," Mara sneers.

"Skank," Rebecca sneers.

"I don't exactly know what you want, Mara, but you made it clear where we stand. So while this is fun and all, I need to grab a cup of coffee before my next class," I say, breaking the tension.

Mara attempts to say something else, but I don't have time for it. I grab Rebecca's arm and drag her away.

"Remember, Cassi, you're only as good as the company you keep," she yells to our backs.

"I fucking hate her."

"I know," I sigh, suddenly exhausted.

"She's toxic and wants to be the center of attention."

"I know."

"I seriously don't know why you still talk to her. Anytime you've ever shown an interest in a guy, she's put the moves on him, pushing you to the side. Is that really the kind of friend you want?" Rebecca huffs.

"You know it's not. We aren't even really friends anymore, but you also know I can't just walk away when her mom and mine are best friends. It's easier to keep the peace," I remind her for the thousandth time.

"Can't believe she had the audacity to call herself your best friend." Rebecca rolls her eyes as we walk into the coffee shop. I play on my phone as Rebecca checks out the bulletin board as I go through my emails.

"Hey." She hits my side, getting my attention. "The rodeo is coming to town this weekend. You want to go?"

"Sure." I smile. "I wonder if Xavier has ever been to a rodeo before."

"Only one way to find out." Rebecca raises her brow. "You text Xavier and I'll text Jack." She says as we move up the line.

"So, Jack, huh?" I ask as I type out a text.

Me: what are you doing this weekend?

"I like spending time with him but we're young so who knows what will happen," Rebecca says as she texts Jack.

Avi: Shouldn't I be the one to ask you that? I've got nothing planned, why what's up?
Me: How would you feel about going to a rodeo?

"I get that," I tell Rebecca as I wait for his reply.

We move up to the register and place our orders. My phone buzzes as I pay. Once we move off to the side to wait for our order, I read his message.

Avi: If it means spending more time with you, then I'm game.

"Smooth," Rebecca mutters, reading over my shoulder.

"Hey, no snooping," I chastise.

"Really?" she deadpans right as the barista calls our names. We grab our coffees as I text him back.

Me: Smooth. Better get ready to get your Texas on city boy.

Xavier

I DON'T KNOW what I expected when Cassi invited me to a rodeo, but it sure wasn't this; I think as I take in the fair going on. Flashing lights, rides, and rigged games galore with the scent of fried food lingering in the air.

"I don't know what I was expecting, but it sure wasn't this," I tell her as we walk side-by-side into the fair, trailing behind Jack and Rebecca.

Cassi looks around, nodding. "Yeah, I probably should have mentioned this isn't a normal rodeo."

"What do you mean?" I ask, moving closer to her as the crowd thickens.

"Every year the rodeo and the fair come to town at the same time. Two separate events but you can easily go from one to the other." she shrugs. "Having the two side-by-side increases the turnout."

"Make sense. It's good for marketing."

"Exactly."

"Hey, you two!" Jack yells, getting our attention.

"What do you guys want to do before the rodeo starts?" he asks.

I look at Cassi. "Up to you, I'm along for the ride."

"How about we break up and meet back up at the rodeo entrance in thirty minutes?" Rebecca says.

"That sounds good to me." Cassi shrugs. "That okay with you?"

"Sounds like a plan." I nod.

"Awesome, now Jack," Rebecca says, pulling him away. "Can you use your muscles and win me a stuffed animal?"

"Can I? Psh," Jack says, making us laugh as we watch them walk away.

"They are something else."

"Aren't they?" Cassi says. "So, how about we walk around until we find something that we want to do?"

"Sounds good," I say, reaching down and taking her hand in mine.

I see Cassi duck her head as we walk, but not before I caught the hint of a smile.

Walking around, none of the rides or games catch our attention.

"What do you think about finding a dark spot and making out for a little while?" Cassi asks, brows raised.

I pull her into me, kissing her neck. "I think that's the best idea you've had all night," I rasp into her ear, making her giggle.

With her hand in mine, I lead her over to a spot between two booths and push her up against the railing. I weave my hands into her hair and kiss her. Cassi moans into my mouth, letting me deepen the kiss. Her hands trail up my back, to my neck and into my hair as she rubs her body against mine.

I could take her right here and no one would never know.

"Xavier," she murmurs after who knows how long.

"What do you need?" I ask, kissing her neck, kneading her ass.

"You. I need you." She sighs, arching her back.

"We both know we can't do anything here. Too many eyes."

"No one can see us," she growls, nipping my chin.

As I open my mouth to respond, her watch vibrates with a text.

"Fucking cock blockers," she mumbles, resting her head on my chest in defeat.

"Come on, you don't mean that," I tease as I pull away. "Let's head that way."

"Fine, lead the way," she huffs, acting put out.

I look down at her red swollen lips and mused hair.

I did that. I did that to her.

Clearing my throat. "Should we grab some food to take in?" I ask, pointing to a fried food booth that advertises fried ice cream.

"Oh, let's get some fried ice cream and fried Oreos to eat together," Cassi says breathlessly.

We move, getting into line. Once to the front, we place our order for more food than we will probably eat.

Fried ice cream. Fried Oreos. Fried pickles. Fried chicken.

"Pretty sure I'm going to be working this off for days," I mumble as we walk toward the rodeo doors.

"Pretty sure your abs will live to see another day, Avi," she jokes, making me laugh.

"You guys get enough food?" Rebecca laughs as we approach.

"Pretty sure the guy we bought the drinks from thought the same thing," Jack quips beside her.

"Come on, let's get in there and eat before all this goes cold," Rebecca says, blushing.

Cassi and I follow them into the arena and make our way into the grandstands and find a seat. We sit, separating all the food and eat what we want.

"This is so good," Cassi moans as she dips an Oreo into the ice cream.

"I don't think those sounds are suitable for public," I joke under my breath, making her blush.

"Shut up," she whispers, ducking her head.

"He giving you a hard time, Ace? You're looking a little red," Jack jests, making all of us but Cassi laugh.

"Laugh it up, Jack, just remember payback is a bitch," she jokes.

Once we finish eating, I run the remnants of our meal to the trash can at the bottom of the steps.

"You won't keep her," a guy leaning against the railing says as I approach.

"Excuse me? Are you talking to me?" I ask as I dispose of our trash.

The guy turns and looks me up and down before facing forward again. *Jared.*

"She will come back to me. She always does."

"Are you sure about that?" I ask, crossing my arms.

"We have history. Can't beat history." He shrugs.

"You can if you know the history was bad for you," I say, walking away. Not wanting to listen to any of the other bullshit he wanted to spew.

I look up to see if Cassi has noticed that he's here or not, only to meet Jack's stare. He nods, letting me know we're good and that the night isn't ruined.

"Hey, took you long enough," Cassi teases as I approach.

"Sorry." I smirk, sitting down next to her.

She bumps her shoulder into my side. "You're forgiven just this once."

I wrap my arm around her shoulders. "Don't worry, I won't make that mistake again." I smirk.

The announcer comes over, telling us all to stand for the national anthem, and before I know it, the rodeo is off.

"Hey guys, lean in close. I want to take a picture for social media," Rebecca yells over the crowd.

The four of us lean into the frame and she snaps a few different photos and posts them all.

Guys are thrown, bones are broken, the crowd boos and cheers, and it's like a sensory overload unlike anything I have ever experienced. And the way Cassi gets into it, I can't help but hope this is the first of many rodeos we go to.

CHAPTER NINE

Cassi

Rushing into my dorm, I replay this morning's conversation with Xavier.

"Hey, how about just you and I go do something tonight?"

"Like a date?" I tease, leaning into his side in a booth out of sight.

"Yeah, like a date. That okay with you?" He raises a brow, smirking as he pulls on a strand of hair.

"You won't hear me complain."

"All right. Let me find something for us to do."

"Sounds good." My watch vibrates, reminding me it's time to head to class. "I have to go." I sigh before leaning in and stealing a kiss.

"Take good notes," he says before kissing me once more.

"I'll try," I say as I slide out of the booth. "Later."

"Later."

I toss my bag on the floor and start ripping through my closet.

Wear something old.

That was the text I got an hour ago.

"Hey, what's got you moving so fast?" Rebecca asks as she kicks my bag out of the way.

"Sorry about that." I nod toward my bag. "I'm going out with Xavier."

"Like a date?" she asks, clearly surprised.

"That's what he said," I say over my shoulder as I slip on a pair of jeans.

"You're going on a date with Xavier Walsh and you're wearing jeans?" she says skeptically.

"He said to dress casually. Well, his exact words were something old," I yell, tossing my heads up.

"Okay, okay. No need to freak out. I mean, this is the first real, official date that you've had with this guy that you're clearly head over heels for, but no need to panic." Rebecca throws her hands up.

"That is not helping," I say, rubbing my hands over my face, a little overwhelmed.

"Sorry. Look, you have nothing to worry about, he asked you on a date," she reminds me gently.

"I know." I take a deep breath, trying to calm my nerves as Rebecca scrolls through her phone.

"Can I ask you a question though?"

"Sure," I tell her as I slip a shirt over my head that makes my boobs look fantastic.

"Do you know who babyyates is on social media?"

"No, why?" I turn around and face her.

"I'm sure it's nothing, but she commented about how she can't wait to see him on one of the pictures from the rodeo."

My thumb finds my mouth as I absentmindedly rub my nail against my lip.

Is there someone else? Has he been seeing other women?

Logically, my brain says he spends most of his time with me so when would he have time, but the illogical part says maybe I've been fooled.

"Did you check her profile?" I ask, making Rebecca scoff.

"What do you think I am, an amateur?" she demands. "I stalked her page, and it looks like she has a boyfriend who she is very much in love with, but you never know. I think she's from Chicago or something. She has some pictures from there."

"Huh," I say, pulling my hand from my face, busying myself looking in the mirror. "Avi said before he came here, he was staying in a place called Bridgeton. He said it was close to Chicago. I bet it's just his friend from back home. He's mentioned her a couple of times."

I try to sound confident, but I'm not. As much as we've been together, we've mostly avoided talks of the past. I don't know what happened with this chick exactly, but he let it slip once that he had a thing for her before they decided they were better off as friends.

"Hey, I'm sure it's nothing. But if you're worried, all you have to do is ask Xavier. I'm pretty sure he would tell you."

My phone buzzes and I grab it off my bed.

> **Avi:** On my way up.
> **Me:** Okay.

"He's on his way up," I tell her as I slide my phone into my pocket, grabbing what I need. "It's none of my business. I mean, this is our first official date. Not our wedding."

"Babe, if it worries you, you have a right to know. You guys are friends first and foremost. Don't push your feelings aside because you're scared of the outcome."

I sigh. "I'll think about it."

She narrows her eyes at me, but eventually rolls them. "Fine."

I should have known the word fine coming out of any woman's mouth was a trap, even if she's my best friend. Especially when she jumps, rushing toward the door when he knocks.

"Who's babyyates?" she demands as she opens the door, making Xavier jerk back.

"Rebecca," I chastise.

"Well, hello to you too, Becca." Xavier laughs. "Babyyates? Like the username? That would be Tinsley, my best friend. Why?" he asks, tilting his head.

"She commented on one of our pictures and I got curious. Had to make sure it was nothing for me to worry about." She shrugs. "She's all yours," she tells him, waving at me.

"Okay, then?" His face holds confusion.

"Let's get out of here before she says anything else embarrassing," I mumble, pulling him out the door. As soon as it shuts, I breathe out a, "Well, that was awkward" under my breath.

Xavier laughs, showing he heard me.

"Please pretend you didn't hear any of that."

"Whatever you want." He leans in, pressing a kiss to my lips before grabbing my hand and leading me down the hall.

I don't say anything else until we are in the car. "Tinsley's the one who lives in Bridgeton, Right?"

"Yep. She's actually the reason I even ended up in Texas. You should probably thank her." He looks over and winks at me before focusing back on the road.

"Is she the one you said you had some drama with her boyfriend before?"

He lets out a deep sigh. "Listen, any other time I would tell you whatever you want to know, but right now, I want this to be about us. Can we talk about this later?"

I force a smile. "Of course. I didn't mean to be nosey."

He reaches out, grabbing my hand to pull it to his lips. "That's not what I meant. I don't mind sharing my life with you and I will never feel like you are being nosey. When our date is over, I will answer every question you have about Tinsley and any other ex I have, but while we are on this date, I want you to know I'm thinking about you and only you."

My heart stutters at his admission. "Oh."

I sound like an idiot, but I don't know what else to say.

He gives me a teasing smile. "Yeah. 'Oh.' So let me dote on you Adra."

"I think I can do that."

"Good, because you deserve it. I think you're going to like what I have planned tonight."

Deciding to let it drop and enjoy our evening, I turn in my seat, pulling his hand in my lap.

"Really? Are you going to tell me what it is?" I bounce in my seat.

"No way. It would ruin it. You're going to have to trust that I know what I'm doing."

I pretend to pout. "I mean, I guess, but your game is weak."

He scoffs. "Are you saying I have no game?"

I shrug, hiding my smile. "I'm just saying a goat would probably have better game than you."

"You're going to regret that statement. Especially when you see what I have planned. This isn't even my 'A' game. By the end of the night, you're going to be blown away. I promise."

Leaning back in my seat, I bring his hand up to my lips, kissing it like he kissed mine.

"I can't wait," I whisper to him.

He gives me a bright smile before looking back forward.

I reach up, turning up the radio and sing along to the words. I'm happy to let myself live in this moment for now. Happy to be here with him.

But in the back of my mind, I have a sense of doom on the horizon and it all stems from this mystery best friend.

He hasn't talked about her much at all. Honestly, other than the casual mention in past stories, I know nothing about her. I didn't even know what she looked like until today.

You're being crazy, I remind myself.

Crazy or not, I'm starting to feel like I took a freefall jump. At first, the light-heartedness was exhilarating, but the closer and closer I get to the ground, I feel like I'm out of control. Like I'm falling faster than I can survive.

I just hope I found my parachute in Xavier, ready to help me land safely without getting hurt.

Xavier

AFTER CONVINCING CASSI to go out with me, I had a moment of panic. *Where do I take her?*

So I did what any logical male would do. Call his female best friend.

The video call rang as I drum my fingers on the steering wheel.

"Hey you." Her voice comes through my Bluetooth.

"Hey Tins, how are you?"

"I'm good. What's up."

"What a guy can't call his best friend?" I joke.

"He can, but it's a little concerning when he usually texts."

I groan, rubbing my hands on my face.

"Hey," she says, gaining my attention. "Talk to me."

"I have a date," I tell her. "And I have no idea where to take her."

"You have a date?" Tinsley squeals, shaking the camera. "This is so exciting!"

"Who has a date?" another female voice asks.

"Xavier, and he called asking for advice," Tinsley gushes.

I watch Sage, Tinsley's future sister-in-law, move into screen.

"Ohh, that's exciting. Where are you taking her?" Sage asks, sitting next to Tinsley.

"I don't know," I confess, making her tsk.

"Okay, tell Momma Sage everything. Do you know her favorites?"

I tell her about all the things she's told me about, hoping to spark some sort of idea.

"Wait." Sage smiles, looking over at Tinsley. "Are you thinking what I'm thinking?"

"That would be an amazing date." Tinsley sighs.

"Care to let me in on the idea?"

"Okay, we're going to text you a list of supplies you need to get. You need to find a place to do this, but you're in Texas so it shouldn't be too hard," Sage says flippantly.

"I'll try to find a YouTube link too, so you can see what we're talking about."

I lean back in my seat and breathe a sigh of relief.

I had a game plan.

When I knocked on Cassi's door, the last thing I expected to happen was to be bombarded by Rebecca about Tinsley.

I didn't want it to put a damper on our evening, though. That's why I brushed off the questions about Tinsley from Cassi in the car. I didn't want her thinking about any of that when I was trying to make some new good memories for her.

Truth is, what I thought I felt for Tinsley pales in comparison to what I feel for Cassi. I wish I could pull my head out of my ass and tell her, but I'm nervous.

What if she doesn't feel the same? What if she's not ready for something serious?

I hate that I have these insecurities, but the fear of rejection is real. I could play it off and act cool, but deep down, it scared me to death.

We head about twenty minutes outside of town and the entire time I watch Cassi take quick glances at me.

"Any ideas?" I ask as I pull off onto a dirt road.

"If anything, I have more questions," she teases.

"Good thing we're here." I smirk as I put the car into park.

Cassi looks around at the field surrounding us. "Uh, are you secretly a serial killer?" she asks, making me laugh.

"No, I promise. You're safe. Or you are mostly." I wink as I pop the trunk and get out of the car.

Rounding the back of the car, I grab the trunk and lift it open. I hear her car door open and close.

"What's all this?" she asks, taking in the contents of the trunk.

I open a shallow bucket and lean it toward her.

"Is that a balloon?" she asks, fully confused.

"Not just any balloon. Grab one."

She raises her brow and grabs one. "Now what?"

"Throw it at that tree," I tell her, folding my arms.

Wordlessly, she does as I asked and tosses the balloon at the tree. When it explodes on impact, she gasps.

"Xavier, did you just recreate a movie scene for me?" she asks, wide-eyed.

"Only if you want to. If not, we can get back into the car right now and go find something else to do."

"Hell no. Game on, city boy. I hope you know how to dodge, dip and dive." She smirks, opening another bucket.

"We have three colors each and I also picked up white plastic jumpsuit things if you don't want to ruin your clothes," I tell her.

"Psh, we can put those on before we get back into the car," she says as she slides on a pair of goggles. Looking equal parts ridiculous and attractive.

For the next hour, we throw paint-filled balloons at one another, laughing the entire time.

"Okay, I'm out." I raise my hands, surrendering.

Cassi walks up to me throwing her paint-covered body into mine, leans up and kisses me. I kiss her back, taking it deeper. She moans into my mouth as I nip at her lip.

"We need to stop," I rasp.

"I'm sick of stopping." She growls, making me laugh. "I'm so glad you find this funny."

"I don't find it funny. But I refuse for our first time to be in a field."

"You said that about the beach too. And the library. And the car. See a theme?" She groans.

"I'm sorry, but when I finally ravish you, it's going to be more than a quick fuck. For that, we will need time and space."

Cassi pulls back, looking put out. "I thought city boys were supposed to move fast. Instead, you're moving slower than a tortoise."

"Come on, let's go get something to eat and then maybe go back to my dorm and watch a movie."

Cassi walks backward, toward the car. "Food, then orgasms. I don't care if they are over the clothes Avi, but I need the relief." She smirks.

"I'm sure we can figure something out."

I move to grab a suit out of the trunk. "Wait," Cassi says. "I want to take pictures."

I pull her back to my front and wrap my arms around her neck as she snaps a picture.

"Thanks." She smiles, reaching for a suit.

"Anytime."

Once back in the car, she turns to me. "Can I post this online?"

I give her a funny look. "Of course. Why wouldn't you?"

She shrugs.

I reach out, grabbing her hand. "You can post whatever you want on there. I don't care."

"Okay," she murmurs, pulling her hand out of mine to type on her phone.

Once we make it back to the room, I smile when I see the pizza sitting on Jack's bed. I'll have to thank him.

I texted him while we were on our way back asking him to pick it up, since Cassi was determined to get me alone. She appreciated the thought.

I avert my eyes as she takes off her suit, taking my own off.

"Do you want to change?" I ask her.

She shakes her head. I look at her paint-spattered body, growing hotter as I take it all in.

"What do you want to watch while we eat?" I ask, grabbing the remote, averting my eyes.

She wraps her arms around me from behind, grabbing the remote before throwing it on Jack's bed.

She slides around to the front of me, giving me a wicked smile.

"I'm not hungry anymore. I need something else."

I feel myself twitch with each word she says.

"Oh yeah? What's that?" My voice is raspy.

She leans up, capturing my lips with hers before she kisses along my jawline.

When she starts to pull my shirt up, I stop her.

"Are you sure about this? Once this starts, I won't be able to stop."

Her smile is warm. "I've been wanting this since the beach. Stop being a tease and give me what I need, Avi."

Unable to deny her anymore, I reach forward, pulling her lips to my own. Instead of letting her lead, I push her back until her knees hit the side of the bed. Reaching down, I pull the hem of her shirt until she lifts her arms for me to pull it over her head. Once off, I push her back onto my bed.

"Avi, we're covered in paint."

I chuckle. "I don't care."

I lean in, kissing the parts of her body not covered in paint. The tops of her breasts and across her stomach until I'm at the top of her pants. I unbutton them, glancing up to Cassi's face.

The pure lust on her face is almost enough to knock me on my ass.

I have never had someone look at me the way she's looking at me now. Like she would rather die than go another moment without my touch.

It's powerful.

"Avi, why'd you stop?"

I smirk at her. "Patience, babe. I'm going to make you feel good."

She narrows her eyes. "Less talk, more action. I've been patient for weeks."

Shaking my head, I pull her pants down her legs. She lifts her ass, helping me, eager for what comes next.

I don't do what she expects, though. Instead of continuing to undress her, I move up her body, taking her lips again. When she attempts to move away and take it further, I press harder. When her hands begin to wander, I grab them, pinning them above her head.

"What are you doing?" she gasps when I finally let her up for air.

"Devouring you."

Her eyes darken. She doesn't say another word as I let go of her hands, smiling when she leaves them up. I take my fingers down them, loving the way her skin pebbles with the touch. I don't stop until I reach the line of her bra. When I begin to trace my finger back toward her back, she arches up into me, giving me room to slide my hands behind her while also thrusting the front of her body against mine.

I make quick work of unclasping her bra, using my hand on her hip to ease her body back down.

Her breaths come quicker as I drag the material from her body. As soon as her breasts are free, my breath catches. I lean back, taking in her body.

This woman is the most gorgeous thing I have ever seen. I already knew that, but seeing her naked has only cemented the fact in my brain.

As she lies on the bed, her body bare except for the thin black lace panties covering her pussy, my world freezes. For one moment, I imagine this woman as mine.

Mine.

Is that what I want? To claim her for good?

Then she smiles at me and I feel like my world is right.

Pushing away my thoughts, I lean in kissing her chastely before moving to her breasts.

As I knead one while taking the other in my mouth, Cassi withers beneath me.

Her hands fly to my head, her fingers pulling my hair as she moans.

Glancing up at her, I ask her the most important question.

"Do you trust me?"

"Yes," she breathes out without hesitation.

The smile on my face grows as I move down her body. Gripping her panties, I slide them down her legs, finally letting my eyes fall on the prize.

I place a kiss on the inside of her knee, then inside of her thigh, building the anticipation.

Right when I'm about to dive into her delectable pussy, she stops me with one word.

"Wait."

I feel like my heart is pounding in my chest as I pause, looking up at her. Waiting for her to tell me it's okay.

If she wants me to, I'll stop right now, but I don't know if I'll be able to sit here with her and watch a movie. My body is too wired for that.

"I've never…" She trails off.

I narrow my eyes. "Never what?"

She lets out a heavy sigh. "No one's ever done what you're doing."

I smile up at her.

I'm her first.

Shit, that causes me a sense of joy. Especially since I already knew she wasn't a virgin. It's good to know I'll be her first at something.

Unable to resist, I tease her, "Done what?"

"Don't make me say it," she says, covering her face.

I reach up, pulling her hands away before getting back into position.

"Don't worry, baby. I'm going to eat this pussy right. Ruin it for you so you'll only think of me when you think of it."

Her breath catches. "Please."

The one word comes off as begging.

I don't hesitate a moment longer. I lean in, swiping my tongue along her slit all the way up to her clit. Her moans of pleasure spur me on, making me kiss, lick, and nip until I know each and every place to touch to elicit a response. Once I have a feel for her body, I add in my fingers, knowing it will make her even hotter.

Pressing one finger inside, I feel her immediately clench around my digit attempting to keep it inside.

Her body is primed and ready. It won't take long now. Adding a second finger, I smile when it's a tight fit. She's perfect.

Curling my fingers up, I thrust them in and out, matching my tongue's pace with them.

"Oh fuck," Cassi screams out as he clenches down on me, her legs tightening around my head as her fingers pull my hair.

Her body spasms around me as I continue to lazily lap at her clit as I slow the pace of my fingers.

Once she comes down, she pushes at me, her body shaking.

"What, baby? I'm not done yet."

"Sensitive," she manages out between breaths.

I chuckle, placing one last kiss to her clit before moving up her body.

"This isn't over yet. You said orgasms. Plural. That means I have at least one more to give you."

She lets out a short laugh. "Fine, but only if you let me do something first."

"Oh yeah? What's that?"

She leans up, pushing me to stand before she unbuttons my pants, pulling both them and boxers down my hips.

My erection pops free, bouncing in front of her face.

I have to admit, it's sexy as fuck watching as her eyes grow wider as she looks at it.

"You can take a picture if you want. I hear it lasts longer," I tease.

She gives me an unamused look before leaning forward. Then she takes away my ability to think.

As soon as her mouth seals around my dick, my body involuntarily surges forward.

She gags, but recovers quickly, sliding back to take a breath before going forward again.

She finds a comfortable pace, her hands resting on my thighs as she takes me deeper with each stroke.

"Fuck, Adra. Your mouth is heaven," I groan out, looking to the ceiling, praying I don't blow my load too quick.

Cassi has other plans though. She begins to lightly graze her teeth along my length as her nails dig into my thighs.

The pressure is enough to cause the tingling sensation to travel up my spine.

"Fuck, I'm about to come," I warn her, attempting to reach down and pull her off, but she latches on.

Two more passes and I blow. She swallows every bit of my cum, wiping at the side of her lips when she's done.

"There. The score's tied." She smiles at me.

"Oh, we're making this a competition now?"

I move toward her, pushing her back on the bed.

She shrugs, a playful smile on her face.

"You little minx."

"You love it."

"I do."

I press into her, leaning down to nip at her nipple. She squeaks before moaning.

"What are you doing?" she asks as I continue my assault.

"I'm going for gold, baby," I tease, blowing on her nipple.

I give her other nipple the same attention before moving up her body. As I lay a wet kiss on her collarbone, she arches into me.

"Avi," she whimpers.

Leaning forward I kiss her. "What do you want?"

"I want you inside of me."

I pull back and lean over to the nightstand, looking for a condom, Cassi strokes me, making me hiss. "Are you ready?" I ask as I roll the condom on.

"So ready." She sighs.

I go in for another kiss as I settle over her. We break the kiss and I stare down at her as I push inside. Cassi gasps as her pussy flutters around me, making me groan. I hold still, trying not to lose it.

"Shit, you're so fucking tight," I rasp.

"Move, Avi," Cassi says as she bucks her hips into me.

I begin at a slow pace, loving the way she feels around me. Grabbing her under the knee, I lift her leg higher, making her gasp.

"Faster," she demands, breathlessly.

I pick up my pace as she starts to pull my hair and scratch my back. I feel her fall over the edge and take me with her. I grunt as I shoot my release.

Wrapping my arms around Cassi, I roll us over, her on top of me. "Next time, I'll last longer," I quip, making her laugh.

"You'll get no complaints from me," she says as she kisses my chest. "I should get cleaned up."

"Okay." I let her up, knowing she's right but hate letting her go.

Soon. I can hold her longer soon.

CHAPTER TEN

Cassi

"Hey, your phone just went off."

I watch as Xavier continues to fold laundry, not paying any attention to his phone.

"Will you grab it and tell me what it is, please?"

"Sure." I reach over and grab his phone off the desk and swipe to unlock it. "You should really have it password protected."

"Eh, I do on what's important." He shrugs.

I look down and open the text.

Tinsley.

I frown.

"It's Tinsley," I mumble.

"Ah, what does she want?" he asks casually.

He doesn't know what even seeing her name does to me.

"It's a picture of her with a milkshake and she asked are you jealous?" I tell him, trying to rein in my anger.

Who does this bitch think she is?

"Ugh, that means she's at Momma's House," he says wistfully.

"What the hell is Momma's House, and why is she hitting on you?" I grit out, unable to hold back anymore.

Xavier laughs. "Momma's House is a diner. And trust me, Tinsley isn't hitting on me. Your jealousy is cute though."

"What the hell is that supposed to mean?"

"It means you have nothing to worry about." He drops the shirt back into the basket and sits on the bed, facing me. "Tinsley is unapologetically in love with her boyfriend. You have no reason to worry," he says reassuringly.

"Was there anything ever between you?"

He sighs. "What do you mean?"

"Did you two ever do anything? Were you in love with her? Because I'm sorry, I have a hard time believing all you've ever been is friends with someone as beautiful as her," I say harshly.

"I don't see why this matters." He frowns.

"It matters to me. You've been avoiding this conversation. It's time we've had it."

I meant it too. While our sex life has been off the chain, he is still reluctant to talk about her. That can only mean one thing, but I need to hear it from him.

"You want me to be honest?"

"Yes," I demand.

"Okay, Tinsley and I have always been friends first. When we met, our fathers pushed us together. They saw it as a business deal. What they didn't see is that Tinsley already knew who she wanted to be with. Did we try dating to please our fathers? Yes. Did it work out? No. Did we kiss? Yes, but if I recall the line, it felt like kissing a sibling was tossed out." He raises a brow. "You. Have. Nothing. To. Worry. About," he says, slowly.

"And her boyfriend is fine with her talking to you, a guy she's kissed?"

"Fin knows he's the only one who has her attention." He laughs. "The dude is cocky as hell. We might not be each other's favorite people, but we respect that we both mean something to Tinsley." He stands and grabs another shirt. "Now can you please stop trying to pick a fight? You have nothing to worry about," he says as he folds the shirt and adds it to the pile.

I set the phone back down onto the desk and take a deep breath. He says I have nothing to worry about, but why do I feel like I do?

"You're right. Sorry. I think I need some fresh air."

I stand, moving from his bed, but he grabs my hand, pulling me back.

"Babe, tell me what's wrong."

"Nothing. You said you have nothing going on with her and I believe you. Besides, it's in the past, right? It's not like she's right here."

"Even if she was, you wouldn't have to worry. I don't think about her like that anymore. She's my friend. Nothing more."

"Is that why you asked her to plan our first date?"

His eyes widen. "What?"

"When I posted that picture of us from the field and tagged you in it, she commented on it. She said something like she knew I would love it and that you were doing good. So did she plan it?"

"No. Not really. I was having trouble figuring out where to take you that would mean more than dinner and a movie. I called her to ask for her advice. Hell, her and Sage helped."

Adding the third girl's name isn't helping my temper, it flaring worse with each moment.

"Why didn't you tell me?"

"You were already so worked up about her, I figured it was best not to mention it. I'm sorry that you think I didn't plan that date, but I did. They only helped lead me in the right direction. All the work? That was all me. I didn't even see the comment or I would have explained it then."

"I deleted it. I didn't want to taint the memory."

"Listen." He leans in pressing a kiss to my lips. "We can keep arguing about this, but at the end of the day, I can't change the past. Yes, we had a very minor thing, but it's over now. It has been for a long time. Long before you. She's still my friend, though. I won't stop being her friend just like as much as Finley may hate it, she won't stop being mine."

"I didn't say you had to stop being her friend."

He throws up his hands, turning from me. "I don't know what you want from me. What can I say to make this better?"

A real commitment, I think to myself.

I can't say that though. He said from the beginning he didn't want serious. Until he makes that decision, I'm stuck in the friends with benefits circle.

"Right now? Nothing. I just need some time to myself. I'll call you later?"

He lets out the breath he was holding, turning to me before pulling me in. He presses a kiss to my lips.

"I'll be here. No matter what. Take all the time you need."

Walking out of his room, I can't help the dread that fills me. I feel like our relationship is a ticking time bomb. One wrong move and it can detonate and destroy everything.

I don't think I would survive it either.

Xavier

IT'S BEEN TWO weeks and I don't know what's going on with Cassi. Ever since the day she read the text from Tinsley, she's been distant.

Sure, she is still spending time with me, but it's different. Sure, we still kiss and have sex, but when it's done, she makes excuses of why she has to leave.

It's killing me.

I've tried talking to her about it, but she's made it clear she doesn't want to discuss it.

Part of me wants to ask Tinsley what to do, but the other part feels like that would be a betrayal to Cassi.

When did my life get so complicated?

"You look like you're sucking on something sour. What's wrong, bud?" Jack pauses his game, looking at me.

"Nothing."

"Ah. Girl problems."

I throw a pillow at him.

"Hey, don't be mad at me because you ignored my advice."

"What advice was that?"

He chuckles. "I told you that Ace was one of them girls. You went after that anyway. Now you're fucked."

"That's not what this is."

"Sure, that's why you're here moping on your bed instead of being out with the sexy as fuck firecracker of a girlfriend of yours. Just admit it. You fell for her."

"She's not my girlfriend." I swallow hard at the admission. "We never put labels on it."

"I see. Well, since that's the case, you wouldn't mind if I take her for a spin?"

I jump off the bed, punching him hard in the arm.

"Ow, what was that for?"

"Being an idiot."

"I'm just saying. Stop playing games and claim her. We both know you want to."

"It's complicated."

"Really? That sounds like a line a woman would use."

"Fuck you, man. You asked."

He shakes his head. "Fine. Let's have a pussy ass bitch session. Tell me what makes it complicated."

I debate not telling him, but in the end, I need someone's advice.

"She's jealous of Tinsley. Plus, I don't think she's resolved anything with that Jared guy. It's a mess."

"First." He holds up a finger. "Of course she's jealous of Tinsley. The girl is your best friend, but even if she wasn't, it's in women's DNA to be jealous of other women snooping around their man. Think about it this way, if Cassi had a male best friend, do you think you could be so calm and collected about it?"

I think over his words. Even the thought of another man being close to her makes my skin itch. "I would if she said they were just friends. I would trust her."

"Well, it's obviously an insecurity of hers. You should talk to her about it."

"I've tried."

"Try harder, man. Life isn't easy. It takes work. Now onto my points." He holds up a second finger. "Number two, you have your own insecurities. Why are you even still worried about Jared, man? I haven't seen them around each other in a long time, man. That girl spends all of her time here with us or with that sexy friend of hers. It's obvious to me it's over, so why are you still stuck on it?"

"Past experience and before you ask, no, I don't want to talk about it."

"Whatever, man." He holds his hands up. "Sounds like to me you need to stop comparing Cassi to your past. She's her own person. Until she gives you reason to believe otherwise, you need to treat her as such."

"I guess."

"Good. Now, are we done with all this feelings bullshit? I need you to pick up a controller and help me beat this kid's ass. I swear he's probably a fourteen-year-old, but the fucker keeps killing me."

I chuckle. "Did you seriously only get deep with me because you had ulterior motives?"

"Of course, I did. Why else would I go out of my way to look like a pussy?"

Shaking my head, I pick up the controller. "I hope you get knocked on your ass one day."

CHAPTER ELEVEN

Cassi

My worst nightmare is here and standing in front of me.

For the past two weeks, I've been stuck in a funk. My head has been overanalyzing everything with Xavier. Part of me wants to tell him I need more from him. I need a commitment, but then the other part says I'll lose him if I push too hard.

So when he told me his best friend, Tinsley, was coming to town unexpectedly, I reluctantly agreed to meet him in the quad so he could introduce me to her.

It was a mistake.

Watching him laugh and hug this gorgeous girl is hell on my confidence. The girl is so glamorous. She fits into his world better than I could ever hope to.

They both turn toward me, so I try my best to mask my face. I must not do a good job because Xavier gives me an odd look.

"Tin, this is Cassandra, we're, um..." I don't miss what the silence says. We are complicated. "Friends. We're friends. Cassi, this is Tinsley. She's my best friend."

I internally cringe as she reaches forward hugging me, but I manage a small pat on the back and smile.

"It's so great to meet you. Xavier has told me so much about you. I'm only here until tomorrow, but maybe we could do dinner together? I'd love to get to know you better."

The peppiness and sincerity in her voice makes me want to puke. Or punch her. Maybe both.

Okay, not really. Any other time, I think I would love to be friends with this girl. She seems sweet, but there's one slight problem with her.

Not that she's gorgeous, or that she's sweet. No, the problem is she holds Xavier's heart in her hand even if she doesn't know it.

I can see it in the way he hugged her tightly. Or the way his eyes lit up like a Christmas tree when he saw her.

My heart aches at the love he holds for her.

I want that. No. I need that, but I want it from Xavier.

Fuck, I'm in deeper than I thought.

"I have to get going. I just remembered I told Mara I'd help her get ready for a date tonight."

Another odd look crosses Xavier's face.

He knows Mara, and I have been on the outs, but I couldn't tell him I was going to meet Rebecca. I could see her across the quad with Jack.

Xavier steps closer, pulling me in for a hug, but his arms remain stiff. "I'll call you later?"

"Sure. I might go to bed early though."

He attempts to lean down for a kiss, but I pull back.

Before he can respond, I hightail it out of there like a damn coward.

I absentmindedly rub my chest thinking about them. I can't even be mad about the whole situation. He was honest from the start.

He told me what happened with them. How she chose this other guy over him. I think that's why he was reluctant to start something with me in the first place. I had my own baggage that seemed awfully similar to hers. The difference is, I chose him. She didn't.

I was the idiot who believed that he chose me too, but seeing her, how could he?

Now I'm sitting here looking like a fool while he gets to spend his time with the girl he's in love with, sans the boyfriend he claims she has.

Why is she here anyway?

Xavier made it sound like this boyfriend of hers would be an alpha to the max, never letting her out of his sight. But I didn't see him anywhere today.

Did they break up? Is she here to claim her second prize after tossing out the first?

By the time I get to my room, I've worked myself up. I begin to pace, trying to calm my heart.

Minutes later, the door opens behind me.

"Whoa girl, what's up?" Rebecca asks.

"Fucking men. I hate them." I pace the room.

"I agree, I think. Want to expand?"

"Xavier's best friend Tinsley is here." I stop to face her. "She's a fucking model, Rebecca. She's wearing designer clothes and her hair was laying perfectly even after getting off a fucking plane."

"I see. You're jealous." She smirks, making me scoff.

"Not at all. I'm just giving in to the inevitable. He was in love with her. He admitted it to me himself. He said it was over, but she came here. By herself. Without that boyfriend of hers that he assured me was all over that. Fuck, he could barely introduce me to her. It's obviously his life here in Texas is a dirty little secret. I want to fucking punch him in the throat."

"Whoa. Chill out, girl. Let's not go get violent and end up in jail. Orange is not your color, honey."

I lay back on my bed, huffing. "You're right. He's not worth it."

Rebecca smiles as she gets up from her bed. "That's the spirit. Now the best way to get over a man is to get under another one. This calls for a girl's night out."

"Fuck it. Girl's night out." I jump off my bed, meeting her at the closet.

Rebecca puts on our "getting ready" playlist and by the third song, my heart is lighter. My heart still aches, but it's manageable at least.

Don't think about it. I tell myself.

"Wear this. It will turn heads for sure," Rebecca gushes.

I turn to see her holding out a black dress with intricate ties across the chest. I recognize it immediately. I wore it on Halloween two years ago. Of course, my dad made me cinch up the ties so my chest wasn't showing. He said no one needed to see a half-dressed vampire.

I smile. "This is perfect."

I change into it, loving the way the soft fabric feels on my skin. I tie the front loose before going and looking into the mirror.

I look good. Damn good.

The dress is on the shorter side, which will make dancing a little harder, but I don't mind. This is for me. I'm going to go out feeling gorgeous tonight for me.

I probably won't get under another man like Rebecca suggests, but I sure as hell will dance with a couple.

I'm going to do everything I can to forget Xavier Walsh.

Xavier

"I'VE NEVER BEEN to a country bar before." Tinsley's eyes are wide as we walk through the door.

I smile. I remember it being a culture shock for me as well my first time here. Especially the dancing, which is why I brought Tinsley. She will love the dancing.

We go up to the bar and I order us a couple of sodas before finding a place against the railing surrounding the dance floor.

"Oh, my goodness. Look at how they move. It's so cool looking," Tinsley gushes.

I see Virgil talking on the other side of the dance floor. Finley's going to hate me, but Tinsley is going to love it.

"Just wait. You haven't seen the best yet. I'll be right back."

I walk over to the man, standing to the side as to not interrupt their conversation.

"Well, don't be shy, son. Come on over here." He gestures.

I walk closer and hold out my hand. "Hello, sir. My name's Xavier. I have a favor I would like to ask of you."

He gives my hand a firm shake. "Virgil. What is it you need?"

"You see that pretty girl over there?" I point toward Tinsley.

He looks over with a smile. "The pretty young brunette over yonder?"

"That would be the one. It's her very first time in Texas and I was wondering if you would dance with her. She would love it."

He pats me on my shoulder. "It would be my pleasure to give your young lady a stroll on the dance floor. You're a good man. Not many men are willing to let their ladies dance with another fella."

I laugh. "Oh, she's not my lady. She's a friend visiting from out of state."

He chuckles. "Are you trying to put yourself out of the game before it starts?"

"Nah, her game's not the one I want to be playing," I say, thinking about Cassi.

He gives me a wink. "Noted. Well, how about I go show your lady friend how us men in Texas do things. Maybe make her want to move here."

I laugh. "Thank you."

We walk over to Tinsley together, her eyes questioning as we approach.

"Tinsley, this is Virgil," I say, stepping up to her side.

"Well, hello there, little lady. I was wondering if you might fancy a stroll on the floor with me?"

I smirk at her when she looks up at me, not sure what he just said, knowing he's putting it on extra thick just for her.

"He wants to dance with you. Go." I push her off her stool.

"I don't know how to dance to this." Her eyes now wide with fear.

"Don't you fret. By the time we're done, you'll be the envy of everyone in here. All the guys will want to dance with you while the girls will wish they looked as good as you out on that floor."

Virgil's a smooth talker, that's for sure.

She gives me one last look before sliding her hand into his and letting him lead her to the edge of the dance floor. They talk a little as they wait for the next song to come on. Once it does, he pulls her out, placing her left hand on his shoulder, while taking the other in his hand.

Then they are moving.

My mind goes back to seeing him dance with Cassi. She made it look effortless. She looked gorgeous under the dim lights as he twirled her around the floor. Like she was born for this.

The dance with Tinsley is similar, but not as complicated. He keeps the steps simple, moving her easily across the floor. Before I forget, I pull out my phone, recording them.

Once they are done, she gives Virgil a hug before coming back to me.

"Oh. My. God. That was so much fun! I want to do that all the time." She takes a long swig of her soda.

"I'm sure if you ask, he'll keep dancing with you. He's kind of known for dancing with the ladies."

She chuckles. "Oh, I plan on it."

"You should send this to Fin." I motion toward the video now playing on my phone.

She laughs. "He will love that. Send it to me."

"Have you talked to him?" I ask casually.

She sighs. "He won't tell me what he had to take care of, but he assures me he's safe and that he wanted me away from it all. I knew when he stopped working for Rocky that he would owe him a favor."

"It must have been a big one for him to send you out here. He hates me."

She swats my arm. "He doesn't hate you. Finley trusts you. He knew I would be safe here with you and you wouldn't let anyone mess with me."

"Well shit, now that you say that, you better delete that video or else he will never let you visit me again." I try to grab her phone, but she pulls away.

"No way! I'm sending it. You already sealed your fate, buddy."

"Damn, X, you've been holding out. Who is this dime piece?" I shake my head as I turn to greet Jack.

"Hands off, Jack. This is my best friend, Tinsley, who is off-limits."

He places his hand over his chest. "I'm wounded. Why would you put someone as pretty as her off-limits?"

I push his shoulder. "It's not me putting her off-limits. She has a psychotic boyfriend who wouldn't think twice about burying your ass, and then I would likely get a shitty ass roommate. I'm simultaneously saving your life while keeping mine pleasant."

"Hey," Tinsley protests. "I can handle myself." She reaches out her hand. "Nice to meet you."

He looks at her hand with wide eyes like he's afraid, but then he smiles, shaking her hand. "Nice to meet you too, ma'am."

"Ma'am? I'm not eighty." She rolls her eyes.

"That's what we call all the pretty ladies down here. Speaking of pretty ladies, X, did you know your girlfriend is on the other end of the bar in a sexy little get-up getting all the guys riled up?"

My heart races. "Cassi's here?"

"Funny, I thought she wasn't your girlfriend?" Tinsley quips.

"It's complicated," I mumble.

"Well, complicated or not, let's go say hi." She gets off her stool, but I wave her off remembering the look on Cassi's face earlier.

"Let me talk to her first. I'll be right back. Jack, will you keep Tins company?" I give him the look that says this is serious.

"Of course. Go get your girl."

I walk toward the end of the bar, spotting her instantly.

Fuck, does she take my breath away. She's a walking wet dream. In a black, lace dress that barely covers her ass, her legs look sexy as fuck. She has her hair curled, falling across her back, ending just above the hem of her dress. Her tan legs peek at me between the material of her dress and her high, cowgirl boots. She looks like she just stepped out of a country music video.

The group she's with burst out with laughter, shaking me from the trance she pulled me under.

Walking up to her, I let my hand fall to the small of her back as I whisper in her ear, "Fuck, you look sexy as hell right now. I could just eat you up."

She stiffens. "Xavier, what are you doing here?"

Her voice is emotionless, which tells me that look I saw earlier was something.

"Tinsley invited you to come with us. You said you were busy." I can feel myself getting defensive.

Why is she acting like this?

"I guess I just assumed this wasn't her scene." She gestures to the table that has gotten eerily quiet.

"Can we go somewhere to talk?" I change tactics.

"Nope, I'm busy. Run back off to your little girlfriend," she dismisses me, turning back to her friends.

It's on the tip of my tongue to tell her my girlfriend is sitting in front of me, but before I can say a word, one of the guys from the table stands up, offering his hand to her.

"I would love to dance, Ian," she answers his unasked question, getting up from her stool.

Seeing her hand in his snaps something inside of me. Before I know what I'm doing, I pull her from his grip, placing my body in front of hers.

"Get your hand off my girl," I grit out.

"Sounds like she doesn't want to be your girl anymore. Take the hint, buddy." He tries to step around me, but I sidestep to block him.

Cassi pushes me back. "Get away from me, asshole."

"No," I say over my shoulder. "You're not going with him."

"Oh, and who is going to stop me?"

"Me. Your boyfriend. Now we need to talk." I turn, facing her, but her face is pure fury.

"I'm not going anywhere with you and you're not my boyfriend. You made that abundantly clear earlier with your size two model."

Fuck, she's feisty when mad, but I'm not deterred.

"That's not what that was. We need to talk."

The man, Ian, reaches around me, gripping Cassi's arm, pulling her around me.

I don't hesitate. I let the red take over, throwing my fist until it connects with his face.

Within seconds, he goes to swing back, hitting my cheek. I don't hesitate, surging forward until I see Cassie step between us. I stop immediately, but he doesn't. He continues forward, swinging as he comes.

I see the second he realizes that Cassi is screaming in front of him, but he can't stop his momentum.

I can, though. I pull her into me, turning, feeling his fist connect with the side of my head. My ear rings as I keep her in my arms, shielding her with my body.

Then a bouncer is beside me, pulling me away. She walks behind us screaming as I'm pulled from the bar.

Outside, they separate us, telling us both to chill out while they figure out what happened.

Tinsley and Jack come rushing out, adding to the tension.

"What happened, Xavier?" Tinsley cries, her eyes wide as she takes in my appearance.

"This fucktard thought he could put his hands on my girl." I nod to Ian, who has his own group of friends surrounding him.

"I'm not your girl," Cassi grumbles from beside me.

I don't miss the fact that her friends are with Ian, but she's beside me, running her hand along the side of my face and under my eyes.

I wince slightly at the pressure she applies.

"It will bruise, but I think you'll be okay." She goes to move away.

I grab her hand and press a kiss to it. "Don't go."

Her eyes waiver for a moment, then she nods, pulling her hand out of my grip.

We all stand quietly until the cops pull up.

I hand my wallet, phone, and keys to Cassi. I tell her the PIN to unlock my phone and my pin to pull money from the ATM.

"If you have any trouble, call my dad and tell him what happened. He won't be happy, but he will get you whatever you need to get me out."

Cassi looks up at me with an odd look before handing my stuff back. My heart drops, ready to repeat the information to Tinsley, but Cassi meets the cop as he heads our way.

"Hey, Earl," she says.

"Cassandra. I didn't expect you to be involved with this. What's going on?" The officer glances over at me as I stand and move toward her.

"A misunderstanding. They are both cooled down now. We're going home anyway. There won't be any more problems."

He gives her a disapproving look. "Was the disagreement over you?"

She frowns. "Why does that matter?"

"Well, young lady, dressed like you are, I'm not surprised that two fellas are in a fight over you. What are you wearing? Your father won't be happy when he finds out."

I wrap my arm around Cassi, pulling her into my side. "Are you saying that there's something wrong with the way she's dressed, sir?"

He meets my eyes with a glare. "She shouldn't be parading herself around in such little clothing. She's just asking for trouble."

I go to speak again, but Cassi beats me to it. "Earl, are you saying that because of the way I'm dressed that something bad might happen to me? That's a very closed-minded way of thinking, isn't it? Inferring that if something were to happen, it would be my fault? I'm sure my daddy would have a few words to say about that."

"Well, that's not what I said now. Don't you go putting words in my mouth." He rubs the back of his neck that is noticeably redder. "Look, I need to talk to the boy over there, but if his story matches up, you'll be free to go."

We go back to Tinsley and Jack, waiting twenty minutes before they let us go with a stern warning that if they get another call, we will both be escorted out with cuffs.

No worries there because we are leaving.

"Come on, Cass. I'll take you to your dorm." I grab her hand, but she pulls out.

"This does not mean we are okay. I can get my own ride home."

I growl.

Tinsley steps in. "Jack's going to give me a ride back to my hotel. I'll text you when I'm safe in my room. Cassandra, it was a pleasure to meet you. I hope we can get to know each other better next time we meet."

Tinsley doesn't wait for an answer, squeezing my arm before she leaves with Jack.

"You're going to let him take her home? I thought you would want to do that."

"She's not my concern, Cass. You are. Please get in the damn car so I can take you home."

She huffs, but gives in. Once she's inside, I rub the side of my face that is throbbing before I get in beside her.

I drive toward her dorm, the silence in the car stifling.

"You really gave me your phone code and pin to your card? Why?" She finally breaks the silence.

"I trust you," is all I reply.

"Why did you do that? I never took you for a bar fight kind of guy."

"I'm not, but I won't let another man touch what's mine."

"I'm not yours, Avi. We had some fun, but you were always reluctant to put a label on it. What's changed now?"

The tightness in my chest lessens with her use of her nickname for me.

"I don't know," I tell her honestly. "But I know that I'm not letting you go."

She doesn't respond, and I don't say anything else either.

I've never done anything that might land me in jail, but tonight I did. Seeing that man with his hands on her took all sense from my head. All I could think of was getting her in my arms and out of his.

Jealousy.

I was jealous.

This recent development has changed my perspective of everything that has come before.

I've had girlfriends before. I'm not a saint either. I've had sex, but never once did I feel the way I felt tonight.

If they left me, oh well. The one that cheated? Fuck her. She wasn't worth it.

Hell, Tinsley's the only one who ever came close to making me feel this way, but it never was jealousy. I felt like I needed to protect her. My pride was wounded when she chose Finley, but I easily accepted him when I saw how happy he made her. Well, that and when I realized he got his head out of his ass and would appreciate her the way she deserved.

Not with Cassie. I don't think I could let her go, even if she was happier without me. I don't think I could stand seeing her happy with another man.

We pull up to her dorm and I park, still lost in my thoughts.

"What are you doing?" she asks, shaking me from it.

"Walking you to the door. Making sure you're safe," I say before getting out and walking around to open her door.

Once she's out, I stay by her side, walking her to the door. Instead of the front door, which is where I was leading her, she grabs my arm leading me around back. Once at the back door, she stops and looks at me.

"I'm not sure how I feel right now. I need time to process, but I want you to come up to my room so I can look at your eye. Then you leave. Agreed?"

I smile at her concern. "I'll be okay. You don't have to worry about me."

"Yeah, but I am anyway. For my peace of mind, come up."

It's more of a demand than a question.

She's quiet as she leads me up the back stairs. She pokes her head into the hallway both ways before she waves me forward.

Once in her room, she closes the door, gesturing for me to sit on one of the beds.

"Sit down. I'm going to get some ice. Be right back," Cassi says as she exits the room.

I haven't been inside her dorm before. One side is messy. Clothes balled up on the floor at the end with an unmade bed and an old drink and candy on the end table. The other side, the side she gestured me to, is immaculate. Bed made, not a stitch of clothes anywhere and nothing, but a photo of Cassie and another man on her dresser. There's another photo of her and the man, along with two older people hanging on the wall.

Her family.

You can see the resemblance between her and Ryan. She looks like a younger version of her mother.

Cassi comes back with ice in a paper cup, setting it on the nightstand. Then she moves to her closet, pulling out a washcloth.

Wrapping a couple of pieces in the washcloth, she moves closer to me. I spread my legs so she can move even closer as she looks at my face.

"It's going to bruise pretty bad, but the ice should take some of the swelling down." She carefully presses the washcloth to my face.

"Thanks," I mumble, not really caring about the ice, but not willing to give up her being here with me.

"I can't believe you punched that guy," she mutters.

"I would do so much more than just punch a guy for you, Cass."

Her eyes meet mine and I see them soften a little.

"Well, how about we not worry about that? I don't need you going to jail for me. Besides, I agreed to dance with him."

I bring my hands up to her hips and pull her into me, resting my head on her stomach. She squeaks, but doesn't stop me, even though it prevents her from icing my face.

"I know, but I couldn't…" I trail off.

She lets out a heavy sigh, burying her free hand in my hair. "I got it. You know I felt the same way seeing you with Tinsley today."

"I never want you to feel that way. She's just a friend."

"How am I supposed to feel when I see you light up seeing her and then finding out her possessive as fuck boyfriend didn't come with her? It's suspicious."

I pull back, looking up into her eyes. "He got into some shit back home and sent her here to keep her safe while he deals with it. Trust me, he's not happy about it. But he wanted her safe. He's going to be pissed when he finds out I let Jack take her back to the hotel and I didn't do it myself. I don't give a fuck though. Jack's a good guy, and she's safe. I needed to be with you. He would've done the same had the roles been reversed."

She frowns a moment before pulling out of my grip, setting the washcloth and ice on her nightstand.

"Maybe you should go," she whispers.

"Please." I reach out, grabbing her hand. "Let me hold you for a little while longer."

She looks at our hands for a moment. "Okay."

She pulls out of my grasp to grab some clothes, excusing herself to the bathroom, taking the ice with her. When she comes back, she throws her dirty clothes in a hamper in the closet before making her way back to me.

I take in her appearance. In the black dress was sexy as fuck, but she looks even sexier now in a pair of sleep shorts and a tank top with her hair piled on her head and a face free of makeup.

Fuck, this girl would look sexy in a damn potato sack, I'm sure of it.

"Take off your shoes and move over."

I do as she asks, watching as she climbs into her twin-sized bed beside me. She pushes me until I'm lying on my back, pressing her face against my chest. I don't hesitate, pulling her into my body, letting her wrap herself around me.

I lean down and kiss the top of her head before running my hand up and down her shoulder.

"You can only stay a little while. We aren't allowed to have boys sleepover," she mumbles.

"Okay. Only for a little while. Got it."

Then there's silence. I listen to her breaths until they even out and I know she's asleep. I consider getting up then, but I don't want to wake her.

Just a little while longer.

I tell myself as I let myself drift to the comforting sounds of her breathing.

CHAPTER TWELVE

Cassi

Everything wasn't perfect with us, but Xavier and I had taken a step in the right direction.

There are times when I still feel like I'm walking on eggshells around him when it comes to Tinsley, but that's my issue, not his.

I need to come to terms with my own feelings and learn to move on from them. Tinsley isn't a threat to me.

Xavier made that clear when he chose me over her.

"Adra, my beautiful girlfriend. What are you doing?"

I smile as I feel his breath fan across my face.

"What does it look like I'm doing?" I whisper.

He glances down at my book before pressing a kiss to my cheek. "Haven't you studied enough? Come on. Come play with me."

I look up at him, rolling my eyes, but I know I'm not going to deny him.

I can't help it. Whenever he's near me, I want to be as close as I can to him. I feel like I've become addicted to him. Addicted to the way he makes me feel. The way my blood sings whenever he touches me.

"Okay," I whisper back.

That sexy smirk fills his face as he moves around me to pack my bag for me. I don't even bother trying to help as I watch him. Once my bag is packed, he puts it over his shoulder, grabbing my hand.

He starts to half run through the library, making me giggle.

A chorus of "shhh" echoes out, making me slap my free hand over my mouth. Once outside, he pulls me down the steps and to the side of the building.

Then he presses me into the wall, his lips crashing to mine.

He wastes no time opening his mouth to me, so I take what he is giving me, losing myself in the feeling of him. His hands come up, cupping my face as he presses even closer, a small bite from the brick wall behind me pressing into my head.

Once I'm completely breathless, he finally pulls back, his own breath coming out in a pant.

"What was that for?" I manage to get out.

"I fucking missed you." He grabs my hand pressing it to his hard dick. "I need you, Adra."

I squeeze him, a moan slipping from his lips causing a rush of heat to rush to my pussy. I can feel myself clench around the empty space, begging for his dick to be there.

I glance around, seeing that where we are is shadowed in darkness. I have no idea what time it is, but the sun must have set hours ago, the activity on campus dying down. Not a single person mills about.

Feeling brave, I unbutton his pants. He reaches down to stop me, but I shake my head.

"I need you inside of me right now, Avi."

"People might see," he warns.

I smile. "Isn't it exhilarating? The thought of getting caught."

I didn't know I liked that kind of thing until this moment. As soon as the words leave my mouth, I feel myself growing hotter at the thought. I know if he reaches down, he would feel how drenched my panties are.

"Fuck," he curses. "I don't have a condom on me, baby."

I bite my lips. "I'm on the pill. I trust you. Do you trust me?"

He presses a kiss into my lips. "Fuck. Are we really doing this?"

He asks the words, but his hands give him the answer. They dive down into the back of my yoga pants, gripping onto my ass as he grinds himself into me.

I latch on to his neck, kissing and biting.

"Are you fond of these pants?" he asks.

"Not particularly, why?"

Then I hear it. The rip of fabric as I feel his hands between my legs.

"Those were too thin, anyway. Way too easy to rip." He breathes in my ear as he pulls himself out of his pants.

Before I can say a word, he picks me up, pressing my back against the wall. Then he pushes aside my panties, lining himself up at my entrance.

He looks up at me with lust-filled eyes. Then he thrusts in.

This is the most primal thing I've ever done. All I can feel in the moment is the pressure of him rubbing against my walls as his chest creates the perfect pressure against my breasts.

His pace is punishing, his hands on my hips digging in, causing a delicious amount of sting to go with my pleasure, causing me to climb higher and higher.

I knew I wasn't going to last long the moment he pulled me from the library, but I didn't know it would feel like this.

As I hear voices float to me from somewhere nearby, my pleasure hits its peak, sending me over the edge.

I moan, but before the full sound can get out, Xavier presses his lips to mine, swallowing it as he pistons a few more times before he stiffens.

I can feel the heat of his cum as it pours into me, making me spasm around him.

He holds me against the wall as we both come down, my ears ringing while my brain remains foggy.

I don't know how long we stand there like that, but when the sound of laughter filters to us, we both startle.

I look to the side and see a group of students moving past the front of the building, not paying us one bit of attention.

Xavier doesn't waste any time though. He pulls out, moving my underwear back in place before slowly lowering me to the ground. Once he's sure I'm steady, he puts his dick away, looking down at my pants.

I look down and see the rip he made.

I look up, smiling at him. "Worth it."

He shakes his head, grabbing my bag. "Let's get you to my car before anyone sees you. I might kill a man if he lays his eyes on what's mine."

"Yours?"

He grins at me. "Yes. You're mine."

Fuck if that doesn't make my heart soar.

Xavier

I'm GETTING REAL used to waking up with Cassi in my arms. Every morning she's with me, I wake up and admire her beauty. She's the most beautiful woman I have ever met. Most people want a gorgeous view outside their door, but me? I could live in a box and as long as Cassi is next to me, I would have the most beautiful view.

She's not only beautiful, but she's got an amazing personality as well. Her kindness knows no bounds. She is feisty as well, but not scared to show her more vulnerable side. At least not when she's with me.

I see what Jack has been telling me this whole time.

She's one of those girls that once you meet them, you know they've changed your life irrevocably. I will never be the same.

That's why I have to keep her. I meant what I told her earlier.

She's mine. I refuse to share her with anyone.

She moves, drawing my eyes back to her face. I smile as I see her eyes flutter open.

"Are you watching me sleep?" she asks.

I chuckle. "You caught me."

"I'm really starting to think my original thought of you being a serial killer might have been right on the money."

"Maybe, but keep rocking my world the way you do and you won't have to worry. You'll be safe from me."

She closes her eyes, shaking her head. "You're silly."

Her alarm goes off next to me. I grab her phone, turning it off.

"I need to get up. I told my parents I would be there for breakfast."

"I don't want you to go."

She leans up, kissing me.

"Don't you have to catch a plane or something."

I shrug. "No. I'm staying here."

Her eyes look confused.

"It's Thanksgiving week. You're not going home to spend it with your family."

I look away from her. "My family isn't really like that."

"So what are you going to do?"

"Stay here."

"The dorms are shutting down."

"I got a hotel room, don't worry. I'll be fine."

She leans up, looking down at me. "You're being serious?"

I pull her to me, pressing my lips against hers. "I'll be fine."

She shakes her head. "Of course you will because you're coming home with me. I can't believe you were going to hide this from me."

She slips from bed, pulling on a pair of pants under my T-shirt and her shoes.

"I wasn't hiding it. It just never came up."

"Yeah, because I assumed you were going home."

"You know what they say about assuming."

She huffs, "I didn't think about it. I should have invited you sooner. Get a bag ready, you can stay in Ryan's room."

I get up and walk to her. "It's okay. I'm fine being alone."

"You might be, but I want you to come. Honestly. Please?"

"If you're sure they won't mind."

"They won't. Get packed and pick me up in an hour."

"You're awfully bossy."

She leans up, kissing me. "You love it."

As I watch her walk away, I realize. I think I do.

CHAPTER THIRTEEN

Cassi

"**M**om. Dad," I call out as soon as we walk through the front door.

Dad greets us at the door. He smiles brightly, but it doesn't quite reach his eyes.

This is why I avoided home. I feel guilty for the pain they've felt.

"Hey, Cass. I'm so happy you're home. Is this the young man you said you were bringing with you?"

He wraps his arms around me, looking over my shoulder, I assume staring down Xavier.

I pull back. "Daddy, this is Xavier. He's my boyfriend."

"Xavier, this is my daddy, Jerry."

"Mr. Davis, it's a pleasure to meet you. You've raised one hell of a woman."

My dad instantly smiles, taking Xavier's hand. "Thank you, son. We like to think we did an okay job."

Just then, Mom comes out from the kitchen. "Cassi, you're here."

She walks over to me, also hugging me before turning her attention on Xavier.

"This is the boyfriend." She pretends to whisper to me, but he can hear every word. "He's cute. Good job."

"Hey, woman," my dad warns.

"Oh, hush. It's great to meet you. Why don't you go into the living room with Jerry while Cassi helps me in the kitchen?"

"Of course, ma'am."

I chuckle, knowing he learned that from Jack.

Once in the kitchen, my mom turns to me.

"So how have you been? We haven't seen much of you since school started."

I sit at the counter, watching as she preps for tomorrow's feast.

At least with Xavier here, there will be four people again.

My chest pangs.

"Yeah. Sorry. I've been busy with classes. When I'm not in class, I'm either studying or with friends."

She throws me a small smile. "Or with that boyfriend of yours?"

I nod my head. "Yes. I spend time with him too."

She waves a knife in my direction. "You better be being safe. Not that I wouldn't love to be a grandmother, but it's still a bit early for that."

I cover my face. "Oh my god, Mom. Seriously?"

She throws a towel at me. "Don't take the Lord's name in vain, young lady. I'd hate to have to whoop you in front of your hottie."

"Please don't call anyone a hottie again. That's disturbing."

She laughs. "I'm glad you kept that humor of yours. So tell me more about what's been going on? How'd you meet Xavier?"

I cringe, not wanting to tell her the exact story, but settle for some semblance of the truth. "We met at a party."

"Yeah? Sounds typical for college kids nowadays. You're being safe at these parties, right?"

I can see the worry flit across her face. My heart feels sliced open.

I whisper, "I don't drink anymore."

Her eyes tear up. "I didn't mean it like that, honey."

"I know, but still." I feel my own eyes prick. "I'm going to go give Xavier a tour of the farm. Call me if you need help?"

She nods silently, now lost in her thoughts.

I know the feeling. It's been a while, but I used to get lost in my grief often.

I stop in the hallway, out of view, to press a hand to my chest.

You can do this. You're strong.

I keep saying it until I feel more myself again.

Then I found the man who helped me find my strength.

Xavier

YESTERDAY WAS INTERESTING. Once we got to Cassi's family home, I was ushered to the living room with her father to do 'men things.' Or at least that's what he told me it was when we got there.

What he really meant was sitting there watching some old western on TV while the ladies were in the kitchen.

It felt a bit archaic to me. I would have preferred been in the kitchen with Cassi. Then again, I would have preferred been anywhere with Cassi.

Then she came in and I wanted to pull her into my arms.

She forced a smile while she joked with her father, but she couldn't fool me.

I saw the sadness in her eyes.

So when she asked if I wanted a tour of the farm, I said yes.

I let her lead me around, telling me all kinds of stories of her childhood. Then, when she finally let the tears come, I pulled her into me, holding her until the sun went down.

Dinner was awkward as hell, but mostly because I could see how each of them were caught in their own heads.

If I had to guess, Cassi hasn't been home much lately.

The silence didn't bother me though. I was more worried about Cassi. I could tell she was uncomfortable. That's why I pulled her into her room after dinner.

"Xavier, my daddy will kill you if he catches you in here."

I frown. "I don't think he'd notice, Cass."

She sighs. "I'm sorry. I haven't seen them in a while. I was hoping they were better like me."

"It's okay. No need to apologize. Are you okay?"

She smiles up at me. "I am. Having you here helps."

"Good. I'll always be here then."

"Thank you." She hugs my middle.

I debate my next words, but eventually decide she needs to hear them.

"Have you ever thought about what they are going through? I mean, not meaning you don't know, but you said you were hoping they would get better, but did you consider why you got better?"

She pulls back, looking up at me. "What do you mean?"

"I mean, what changed that made you deal with your grief better?"

She smiles. "I met you."

I shake my head. "I don't think meeting me is going to help your parents, but a change would. I feel like you're tiptoeing around their feelings, scared to make it worse."

She bites her bottom lip. "I feel guilty. I feel like I caused all of this."

"I know you do, which is another topic for another day, but maybe they need some kind of change to help them move through their own grief. Have you considered that they may be careful around you as well?"

I can see her considering my words. "No. I didn't. I've been so caught up in my life, I haven't considered them at all. I've been selfish."

I pull her head to my chest. "Maybe a little selfish, but you were working on you. Remember what I told you before? You can't help someone else if you aren't in the right place to help yourself."

"You're so smart."

"I know."

She pulls back, slapping my chest.

"Do you take your own advice with your parents?"

I avert my eyes, taking in her rooms instead. I smile at the photos on the mirror of her and Ryan. I see a couple with Jared, but I decide not to dwell on them. I'm here with her, not him.

"It's different with them."

"You don't talk about them much."

I trail my finger across the top of her dresser. "Not much to say. They aren't the best parents."

"Do you miss them?"

Shocked by her question, I turn to face her. "What?"

Her eyes are soft. "Do you miss them?"

I think about her question, not knowing how to respond.

"Do I miss them?" I repeat, her head nodding. I let out a heavy sigh. "I miss who they could have been. They were never really parents to me, so to say I could miss them would be a lie. I can't miss something they aren't."

She pinches her lips together. "What if they changed? What if they came and visited you?"

I shrug. "I used to hope that something would bring them home. My graduation, my eighteenth birthday, but they never show. There's always a reason. Before, I would at least talk to my dad, but now that I went against his wishes and came here, he doesn't even talk to me. The only reason I still get my monthly stipend is because of my grandfather. I only met him twice, but he set up a trust fund for me. As long as I'm in college, I can draw from it up until I either graduate or turn twenty-five. If they showed up now, I would want to think they were here for me, but in the back of my mind, I'd be questioning their agenda. It's too late for us, but not for your family. I can feel the love here."

She moves toward me, pulling me into a hug. "I'm sorry, Avi. I'm sorry you went through that and you feel that way. You don't need them though. I'll be your family."

Leaning down, I press a kiss to her lips. "Thanks, Adra."

THE HOUSE FEELS different in the morning. The heaviness from before seems to have evaporated.

I was shocked when I walked into the kitchen to find Cassi and her mother dancing around the kitchen while cooking.

They shooed me out, handing me two glasses of sweet tea for the road.

That's how I found myself sitting on the couch in the living room, watching football with Jerry.

"Have you ever played football?" he asks.

"No, sir. Not really my thing."

"I see. What is your thing?"

I shrug. "I'm going to school to become a teacher. I enjoy playing video games. I like to read."

He nods, never looking my way. "That's good. What did you do to my daughter?"

I sit shocked. "What do you mean?"

Then he turns, smiling at me. "She's not who she was three months ago. She smiles now. She doesn't seem so lost."

I let out the breath I was holding. "I didn't do that. That's all your daughter. She's a strong woman."

"Agreed, but she didn't seem to know that strength until she met you. We haven't talked to her much, but Jared and Rebecca still talk to us."

I attempt to hide my distaste when he says Jared's name.

"Ah, I see you've met Jared." Jerry chuckles. "He's mostly harmless though. He was Ryan's best friend."

The sadness in his tone stops me from snorting at him, calling Jared harmless.

If only you knew. I think to myself.

"He hasn't bothered us in a while."

"That's probably because he can see what I see."

"What's that?"

He smiles. "My daughter is infatuated with you. His complaints would fall on deaf ears."

"I see. Do you have any complaints, sir?" I'm nervous for his answer, but I need to know.

He thinks about it a moment. "I don't think I'll like any guy my daughter brings home, but you aren't so bad."

"Thank you for that. I think."

Then he yells at the TV, ending our conversation, but I didn't care.

I had her father's blessing and while I didn't need it, it sure made everything that much sweeter.

CHAPTER FOURTEEN

Cassi

"**H**ey, Cass."

Walking out of class, the last person I thought I would see waiting for me is Jared. After the last time I went into the frat house and caught him fucking Mara, he's left me alone. I figured that was the end of it, but seeing him now, I know it's not.

"Get away from me, Jared."

I turn walking away, but he catches up to me.

"Wait. Please, Cass. Hear me out."

I shake my head. "I don't need to hear your excuses. I don't care that you slept with Mara, but I do care that it was apparently a setup."

"Please." He grabs my arm, pulling me to a stop.

Sighing, I gesture toward a bench, taking a seat next to him.

"I was going to come over on Thanksgiving, but I saw Xavier's car there and figured I wouldn't have been welcome."

I roll my eyes. "If you were going to cause drama, then you're right. If you were going to come say hi, then you would have been fine."

He shrugs. "I think your boyfriend would have felt differently."

"Is that what you wanted to talk about? My boyfriend? If so, this conversation is over."

"No. No. Fuck." He rubs his hand down his face. "I need to apologize for so much. I don't even know where to start."

"How about at the beginning?" I suggest.

He nods, reaching out to grab my hand. "I am truly and honestly sorry for everything I have ever done to you. You have to believe me. I didn't plan that shit, but I can't say I didn't feel vindicated when I saw the horror on your face. I was high out of my mind. I wasn't thinking clearly, which isn't an excuse, but it's true. I didn't know you were coming."

"Seriously? You texted me."

He shakes his head. "Mara texted you. I didn't know until after you left. She admitted that while I was getting high, she had taken my phone and texted you. Then she seduced me. I knew she always had a crush, but I had always said no out of respect for you. You were my friend. My best friend's little sister. I didn't want to hurt you. Seems I did anyway."

"So Mara set it up?"

He nods. "Not that it matters. I remember smiling at you. I remember you being hurt. I did that, not her. I also made the first mistake."

When I give him a look of confusion, he continues, "The night in the car after the funeral. You were crying so hard. I could feel your heart breaking right along with mine. I didn't know what to do. When I hugged you to me and you clung to me, I liked how it felt. You made me feel something. So then I took your lips, and you didn't stop me. We know how that turned out, but had I kept my distance from the start, we wouldn't have done it."

"You can't blame yourself, Jared. It takes two. It's as much my fault as it's yours."

"Yeah, but Ryan would still kill me if he were here. He would beat the fuck out of me for even considering it."

I chuckle. "He wouldn't be too happy with me either. He'd tell daddy and get me grounded for life."

He laughs along with me before sobering.

"I really am sorry, Cass. I wish I could take back all the pain I've caused you. Know that I mean that from my heart."

"What changed?"

"I think it was seeing your face that last day that did it for me. It knocked some sense into me. After I kicked Mara to the curb, I ran into your friend Jack. He looked ready to kick my ass, but then I kind of just broke down. It wasn't my proudest moment, but he sat with me. After a while, he told me I needed to get my shit together and that if I hurt you again, he would kick my ass into next year. He reminded me so much of Ryan. So the next day, I went home for a couple days and talked to my parents. Now I'm in therapy twice a week, working through some shit."

"That's great, Jared. I'm proud of you."

"Thanks. Anyway, I wanted to make amends. Please say you'll consider forgiving me."

I pull him in for a hug. "You're already forgiven, silly. Your family."

He grips me tight, both of us soaking up that familiar comfort.

"What the fuck?"

The voice causes my heart to stop.

Xavier.

I pull back quickly.

"Avi," I breathe out.

His nose is flaring while his fists clench and unclench.

"I'm going to go. Thanks for hearing me out," Jared whispers, slipping from the bench.

Xavier's eyes never leave him as he strides away.

"It's not what it looks like."

He shakes his head, his eyes meeting mine.

Pain.

I see the pain behind them.

He turns, taking off the way he came. I'm hot on his trail.

"Stop. Damn it, Xavier, stop walking away from me."

He doesn't stop until we're standing next to his car. He turns, leaning against it, waiting for me to catch up.

"You're overreacting. That wasn't what it looked like."

He raises an eyebrow. "So you didn't just sit in there, holding hands with another man? One that you have a history with? Or hug him?"

"How long were you standing there watching?" My anger building at the lack of trust.

"Long enough."

"We were hashing shit out. It wasn't romantic."

He scoffs, "I might have been born at night, but it wasn't last night, Cassi. I saw how you were looking at each other."

"What? How were we looking at each other? With the weight of the grief that we have been holding on to?"

"Lie to yourself all you want. I'm not doing this again. I'm done." He turns to open the driver's door.

I'm furious. This man is so lost in his own world that he can't even see what it's doing to mine.

"You keep putting this all on me. You're so sure that there is more going on between me and him, but you don't see your own hypocrisy. The way you look at Tinsley. The way you smile when she texts or calls. You're still in love with Tinsley. You never truly got over her." The words fly from my mouth before I can stop them.

He slowly turns to face me. "You have no idea what you're talking about. Tinsley's my best friend. There is nothing else there other than the love of a friend. Stop deflecting."

I let out a humorless laugh. "At least I can be honest with myself. Jared was a coping mechanism. It was never about being in love. It was about the comfort we could offer each other. The desire to hold on to the memories of someone we both loved so much that we lost way too soon. A way to handle a grief so overwhelming I thought it would suffocate me. I won't lie to you,

Xavier. I made a mistake in taking that route, but I can move on from my past. You need to grow the fuck up. If you're looking for someone with no baggage. A perfect little princess who has never liked another boy before. Then you're delusional. You won't find her. You'll just end up alone with a list of what-ifs."

When he doesn't speak, choosing to remain quiet, I shake my head.

"Figure your shit out, Xavier."

Turning, I leave him standing there along with my heart.

CHAPTER FIFTEEN

Cassi

"**M**ama?" I call out as soon as I make it through the door.

"Cass, is that you? What are you doing home?"

As soon as I go around the corner and see my mom standing at the kitchen counter wiping her hand on a towel, the tears stream down my face.

"Mama," I cry out, going to her.

She immediately takes me into her arms. "Oh, honey. What's wrong?"

I let myself feel the pain I have been holding off since I left Xavier, feeling my heart crack in my chest. I don't say anything, but Mom doesn't care. She just holds me, rubbing my back while whispering reassurances in my ear.

Once I calm down enough that I can speak without sobbing, I blurt out, "Xavier and I broke up, I think."

"You think?" she asks quietly.

"Gosh, it's such a mess, Mama."

She wipes a tear from my face. "Let me get us some sweet tea and we can sit on the porch while you tell me all about it."

She does as she said, handing me a glass, before leading me to the porch swing. The same porch swing Xavier and I sat on, revealing our secrets to each other not too long ago.

My heart stutters at the memory before I push it away.

Once seated, Mama swings us, letting the silence envelop us while I process my thoughts.

"I feel like I'm dying," I finally say.

"Broken hearts are no fun, but I promise you you're not dying."

I give her a weak smile. "If death is worse than this, then I think I should be more scared of it than I am."

She thinks for a moment, before speaking again. "Death isn't hard on the person who dies. They feel nothing once their heart stops beating. Death is the hardest on those who are left behind. The ones who are destined to relive their deaths and lives over and over, missing them with no chance of getting them back." Her voice cracks and I know she's thinking about Ryan.

Fresh tears fill my eyes as I also think of him. "I miss him."

"I do too, but that's our burden to carry. He's living his best life with the Lord now. Watching over us as the guardian angel he was always meant to be. While we miss him, we also have to be grateful that his pain and suffering is over. He's in a better place and we will see him again."

"I hope you're right, Mama, because I could really use my best friend right now. I hope he's sitting right here next to us, helping me through this."

"Always. He's always with us. I can feel it in my bones." She wraps her arm around me, pulling me to her side.

I rest my head on her shoulder, closing my eyes to feel him too.

"Tell me what happened," she whispers.

"We were doomed from the start. Between the two of us, we have baggage that can fill a jet airliner and then some. I thought we were getting past it, but it keeps rearing its ugly head. I don't think there's any moving past it for us."

"Everyone has baggage. There will always be a past there that you can't change. It's not about your past, but how you move on from it. Do you process it and move on or are you stuck living with your demons? I won't lie, baby girl. I was worried about you for a long time. You spent a long time living with your demons, growing comfortable with them. I wasn't sure if you were ever going to move on from Ryan's death, but I've seen a change in you. Xavier brought you out of that darkness. I know it hurts right now. I'm not saying that you won't scar, but for that alone, I will always be grateful to him. He gave me my Cassi back."

I'm full-on sobbing again, hearing the pain in her voice as she talks about how I was.

"I had no idea you felt that way," I choke out.

"Of course you didn't. It's not like I could tell you. You were so lost in the grief that anything I might have said would have pushed you further away. You were unreachable. All I could do was pray for a miracle. Pray to God that I didn't lose both of my children at once."

Her own voice cracks before we are both hugging and sobbing into each other.

Once we both calm down, I confide in her, "I didn't want to burden you. I felt like I was drowning while watching you and Dad drown too. I couldn't bear losing either of you, so I turned to Jared. He was Ryan's best friend. We leaned on each other for comfort, but I think we started a cycle that was unhealthy. It wasn't until I met Xavier that I really saw it. I would have kept falling into it had he not helped me find a new way. I feel guilty though. Jared is still stuck in it and now he's all alone. I've abandoned him. I feel ashamed that I was laughing and having a good time when Ryan can't be here. When Jared is still grieving."

"I know it's hard to move on. Those feelings are all completely normal, but you have to remember that you are not responsible for anyone else's happiness. You can only control your own destiny. Jared being stuck in his grief is not your responsibility. He can't use you as a crutch to continue to live in it. He needs to find a way out, whether it be from professional help, his faith, or his family. It's not fair of him to latch on to you when you are finally getting your head above water."

I know she's right, but it's hard. It's hard to see the sadness on his face every time I pass him at school. Or see him get shitfaced at a party to cope with his feelings.

"You're right. I know you are," I whisper.

"Darn straight, I'm right. As for me and your dad, I'm sorry you felt you couldn't come to us. We will always be here for you. We were grieving too, but that's no excuse. We should've tried harder to make you feel like we were there for you. For that, I'm eternally sorry."

"Hey, if I need to cut myself some slack then you do too."

She chuckles. "Fair point."

We sit in for a while, watching as the sun sets. It's nice to be here with her, just enjoying the silence.

We both turn as we hear Dad's truck coming up the driveway.

"I guess I should get up and make supper." Mama smiles at me.

"I'll help," I say, standing before helping her up. "I'll meet you in the kitchen."

Heading inside, I hurry into the bathroom, smiling as I hear Dad greet Mama.

"Hello, beautiful. How is it that every time I see you it's like you get even prettier?"

I hear Mama laugh as I close myself in the bathroom.

I want a love like theirs. Forty-five years of marriage and they still love each other.

I clean my face before staring at myself in the mirror. I look better, but I can see still the emptiness in my eyes. For once, it's not because of Ryan though.

No, it's because of this pain in my chest. I rub it as I take a deep breath.

My phone vibrates in my pocket, but I decide I don't want to answer it. I want to be here with my family and forget the rest of it for a while. Pulling it out, I don't look at it as I press the power button until it turns off.

Coming into the kitchen, Dad pulls me into a hug. "Baby girl, what are you doing here? Not that I'm complaining, but isn't it a school night?"

I laugh as I squeeze him a little harder, soaking up the comfort. There is nothing better than a hug from your parents when you're upset.

"It was a hard day. I needed to see my family."

He pulls me back, looking into my eyes. "Who do I need to take to the woods? I'll do it. Just say the name."

I chuckle. "No one, Daddy. It was a bad day, that's all. I love you millions for being willing to commit murder for me though."

"Now, hush, child. It's not murder. It's a hunting accident."

At this, we all burst out laughing. The funny thing is, my chest feels lighter.

"Now, Jerry, get on out of here while we make a quick dinner. Go watch your evening shows." Mama swats at him with a towel playfully.

"Don't you boss me around, woman." He winks.

"Woman? I'll show you woman," Mama says as she starts toward him.

He chuckles, running out of the kitchen, hollering over his shoulder, "Woman? Did I say woman? I meant 'Yes, darling.'"

"That man is going to get it one of these days," she says with a smile.

"You love him," I remind her.

She sighs, her face softening. "I do."

Laying in my old bedroom that night after a laughter-filled dinner with my parents, I let my mind think about Ryan. For once, they aren't the sad thoughts, or the demons as Mama called them. For once, I remember all the family dinners we had. All the joy and laughter.

"I love you, Ryan. I hope you're watching over me."

I say the words, but I can already feel his answer.

I'll always be here for you, Cass.

Xavier

HOURS LATER AND I'm still thinking about Cassi and what she said to me.

You need to grow the fuck up.

At the time, it made my blood boil. How dare she tell me to grow up when she used sex to deal with her grief?

Then I watched her walk away, resisting the urge to pull her back by holding onto my pride.

Laying here in bed staring at the ceiling, I learn a very important lesson.

Pride doesn't keep you warm at night. It doesn't fill the gaping hole in my chest from the woman I have fallen madly in love with.

I'm in love with Cassi.

I sit up straight, finally admitting to myself what I think I've known all along.

I pick up my phone immediately and dial her number. It rings before going to voicemail.

I hang up, trying again, but this time it goes straight to voicemail.

Fuck.

She either blocked me or turned her phone off. One quick way to find out which.

I call Jack. He answers on the first ring.

"What's up, bro?"

"Hey, can you try calling Cassi?"

"You actually want me to call your girl? Is this a test? Bro's before ho's, man."

I would punch him if I could. "Don't you dare call her a ho. I fucked up, man. I think she might have blocked my number. Just try, okay?"

"Stop fucking up, man. Cassi's a great girl. You need to get your shit together or let her go." The stern, lecturing tone catches me by surprise.

"Seriously, man? Like two seconds ago you said you'd pick me over her. Now you're taking her side?"

"Well, yeah. I meant I wouldn't sleep with her or encroach on your territory, but she's a good girl. She's my friend. I won't let you break her heart, man."

I grimace.

Too late.

I'm glad she has Jack in her corner, though. She deserves it, but I can't lie and say it doesn't gut me, it's not me.

"Point made. Now, will you call her?"

"Yeah, man."

He hangs up. I wait for what seems like forever for him to call back.

"Straight to voicemail, man. I texted her though. I'll let you know if she texts back."

"Thanks, man."

I pace my room, thinking about where she might be. I don't stay still long though. Before I know it, I have my keys in my hand, heading to the car.

I go to her dorm first. Rebecca lets me have an earful when she sees me. I don't think she even knows what happened, but she said the fact that I was looking for her and her phone was off meant I must've done something fucked up. I let her lecture me for ten minutes before leaving.

I tried the ice cream shop next. She said once that when she's sad; she likes to come here and have a cone of strawberry ice cream with real strawberries mixed in.

Unfortunately, she must be more pissed than sad because she's not here.

My chest grows tight as I check the bar, the library, and the park and still no sign of her.

I keep trying to call her too. Leaving her messages, begging her to call me back.

I take one last shot in the dark and try the old lake about thirty minutes outside of town. The same one she and Ryan used to go to.

I feel guilty as I pull up to the parking area. For a moment, I don't want to walk down to the clearing. I don't want to taint this place for her. It takes a couple of minutes for me to realize it was pointless, anyway. Her car isn't here.

I get out anyway and travel down the area, remembering the conversation we had. Remembering her worries about this place being altered by others as the popularity of the little lake grows.

I walk over to the tree they marked and run my fingers over their initials.

I feel my phone ding and my heart skips a beat.

I'm disappointed when I see Rebecca's name instead of Cassi's.

> She's at her parents'. Don't make me regret this.

A moment later another text comes through.

> Hurt my girl again and you won't be procreating buddy.

I smile.

> Won't be an issue.

I reply, adding a thanks at the last minute.

I know where she is, now I'm going to go get my girl.

Ten at night. Not late by college standards, but by proper standards to show up to the girl you love parents' house.

I pull into the driveway, taking a minute to collect my thoughts before I get out. Before I get to the door it swings open, a furious Jerry standing in the door with a shotgun.

"What are you doing here, son?" he demands.

"I was hoping to talk to Cassi." I met his eyes, not flinching as he moves the barrel a little lower, almost as if he's considering pointing it at me.

"I don't know what you did to her, but I have no problem making your death look like an accident." His voice is eerily calm.

"Daddy, put the gun down." I let out a breath as I see her.

Cassi. My Cassi.

She's gorgeous as ever in a pair of pajama pants and a tank top. Her eyes look red from crying, if I had to guess. My heart aches at the thought of her crying, but even more so at the thought of me causing those tears.

"Cassi, honey. This is not the time for a young man to show up at your door."

"Daddy, I turned off my phone. He was probably worried about me and wants to make sure I'm okay. You're getting all bent out of shape for nothing."

Jerry relaxes at that, looking back to me. "The threat still stands."

"Heard loud and clear, sir."

Cassi grabs a jacket, before slipping by her dad, closing the door behind her. She doesn't speak right away, stepping off the porch, walking toward my car.

I follow her, almost running into her when she abruptly turns to face me. My hands reach up to grab her arms, steadying her, but she immediately pulls back.

I frown. "Cass, I…" I start, but she interrupts me.

"No. You don't get to do this. You don't get to come here and act all concerned now, when hours ago you were willing to walk away from this. It's obvious to me you don't feel the way I do. If you did, you could've never said what you said."

"Cassi, please," I try again, but stop when she holds up her hand.

"I don't want to hear it." She stops, her voice cracking. "Please, Xavier. Save it. We aren't in a good place. Either of us. I fell for you hard and I'm kicking myself for it. Not because the way I feel for you is wrong, but because I wasn't ready for it. You're not ready for me either. I think we each need to take a breather. Work on ourselves and see where we are after that."

I step forward, cupping her cheek to catch her falling tears. "Babe, please. I don't want that."

She hiccups through a sob. "I don't either, but what we want and what we need aren't always the same thing. I care about you deeply, but we have shit we need to sort, otherwise we are going to keep reliving this cycle or not being able to trust each other's feelings for one another."

I press my forehead to hers as I feel moisture building behind my own eyes. "We can work through this."

"If you ever cared about me at all, Avi, I need you to do this for me. Take time and figure out what you want and what you need. Work through your issues with Tinsley that caused these insecurities. Let me work through my leftover issues from Ryan and Jared. Do this for me."

I whisper, "I know what I need. It's you."

Her tears fall harder. "Please."

"I'd give you anything just to see you smile, babe. Anything."

Even if it means ripping my heart out.

She leans in, pressing her lips to mine once.

"Goodbye."

And fuck if I don't feel like the last nail in my coffin has been placed.

CHAPTER SIXTEEN

Cassi

"How are you doing?"

I didn't expect to see Jack here. My eyes immediately search the library, begging for a glimpse of Xavier.

"He's not with me."

I sigh, but answer his first question. "I'm okay. Really. You don't need to worry,"

"Good. I'm glad one of you is." He runs his hand through his hair.

A pang hits my heart. "He's not well?"

He gives me a sad smile. "He's going through the motions. Studying and going to class, but he doesn't really talk to anyone anymore. I even got a call from Tinsley saying that he's been ignoring her texts."

I sigh. "I can't be responsible for his feelings, Jack."

He nods, a grim look on his face. "You're right. Sorry. I just hate seeing him like this. Changing the subject, how are your classes going?"

I give him a grateful smile. "Good. I'm getting ready for finals next week. What about you?"

He groans. "Don't remind me. I should be studying way more than I am.

I think I may fail humanities."

"I could help you study if you want. I have a humanities class too. I'm sure it can't be too different."

"I've got Owen's, who do you have?"

"Owen's. See, we could totally study together. Then maybe you might not fail."

He chuckles. "You're too good to me. Fine, we can study together."

Rolling my eyes, I smile wider. I missed hanging out with the guys.

I miss Xavier.

I push that thought away.

"When are you available to study?" I ask.

"How about tonight? We can meet at the union."

"Wow, I'll be honest, I didn't think you were being serious."

"I really need the help. Besides, I have a feeling you will keep me focused and make me actually study."

"Bet your ass I will. Can't have you failing a class. I can't be friends with a flunk." I wink, letting him know I'm teasing.

His hand slaps his heart. "We can't have that. How would I ever survive without your sunny disposition and smart-ass comments?"

I shrug. "Hey, with me gone, you might actually win a game of darts."

He gives me a mock glare. "How dare you? You know, back home, I'm the reigning champ at darts."

"Oh, how cute. You know it doesn't count if no one else competes, right?"

He reaches out and pinches me. "You're not being very nice, missy."

"But you still love me." I beam up at him.

He pulls me into a side hug. "I do." Then quieter, he murmurs, "He does too."

I pretend I don't hear, but we both know I did.

I pull back, giving him a smile. "So six?"

He sighs, nodding. "Six."

Xavier

"I saw her today." I glance up at Jack as he comes back into the room.

"Yeah? How was she?" I don't bother hiding my desperation.

At first, I tried to hide it, but Jack wouldn't have it.

He came into the room one day, talking about how my feelings for Cassi must have been fake seeing as I'm was so calm about everything. Then he suggested I go out and find a new booty call.

I had him up against the wall before he could finish his sentence.

Then he laughed.

"There you are. I thought Xavier, the friend I know and love, had been replaced by unfeeling aliens. Now, what are we going to do to get her back?"

That was when I realized not only did I not deserve Cassi, but I don't deserve Jack either.

He's a one-of-a-kind friend. He might be the fun of the party, but he would have your back in a heartbeat.

"She's good, man. She misses you, I think. She didn't want to talk about you, but she's good. I'm going to see her tonight."

I tense up. "What do you mean?"

He shrugs. "She's going to help me study for humanities. I figured I could find out what she's been up to while I'm at it."

I let out the breath I was holding. I shouldn't have doubted him for even a half a second. He's a genuine friend.

"Thanks. Keep your hands to yourself," I add in on a tease.

"It will be hard, but I will. The question is, who is going to keep her hands off of me?"

I jump up to hit him, but he takes off out the door.

"Asshole," I holler at his retreating form.

"You love me." His words flow back to me.

I give a small smile to the other two guys in the hallway, ignoring their questioning looks. Fuck them. They don't get to judge.

I close myself back into my room and return to my spot on my bed to go back to studying.

Hey. The woodshop is going to be open tonight.

I smile at the text from my classmate, Grant. I didn't really know him until two weeks ago, but with enough money, he was willing to help me out on a special project.

What time? I'll be there.

A couple hours later, I meet Grant at the woodshop.

"You sure about this man?" he asks, counting the money I slipped into his hand.

One thousand dollars. The best money I have ever spent.

"Yeah. I took a woodshop class at the academy, but I don't know how to use all the stuff. I want this to look perfect. It's really important."

He nods. "Let's get to work then."

I hand him the haphazardly cut pieces of wood. It's going to be hard, but I'm not willing to give up on this.

CHAPTER SEVENTEEN

Cassi

irPods in, I jam out to some nineties rap trying to study. I found a corner tucked back into the library and haven't seen a person since I sat down. I put my phone on, do not disturb, blocking out the world.

You've been doing that a lot lately, a little voice in my head says.

It's been two weeks since I officially broke it off with Xavier. To say it's been difficult would be an understatement. I still see him occasionally on campus. With Jack deciding to hang around, I sure get enough updates on him.

Truth is, I miss him.

From what Jack says, I know he would take me back in a heartbeat if I just picked up the phone and called him. I can't do that though.

Even though I denied it, I have some messed-up shit to deal with. I thought I was coping with the death of Ryan, but I wasn't. I was hiding from it. Xavier helped me take the first steps toward confronting my overwhelming grief, but I'm not there yet.

If I called him now, I would only be using our relationship as a way to avoid those feelings again. That wouldn't be fair to him or me.

While I hope when I'm ready he is still there, waiting for me, I also know that asking him to do so would be selfish. That's why I had to let him go.

But you love him.

Shaking the thought away, I fall into nineteenth-century America for my history class. I don't know how long I throw myself into it, but I startle when a hand touches my knee.

I let out a gasp, pulling my earbuds out.

"What's up?" I ask a frazzled-looking Rebecca.

"I've been looking for you," she says harshly as she pulls my books out of my lap and jamming them into my bag.

"What the hell are you doing? I'm studying," I hiss, trying to keep my voice down.

"We need to leave," she says, standing with my bag in hand.

"No, we don't, I need to study." I pull on my bag, not moving. "What's gotten into you?"

"I swear to God, Cassandra, I'm sick of your shit. If you want to stay here? Fine, but I'm going to the hospital," she spews, dropping my bag at my feet.

"Hospital? Why are you going to the hospital?" I frown, watching her retreat.

"Because that's where Xavier is and someone needs to sit with Jack," she says over her shoulder.

I scramble, grabbing my bag and chasing after her. "What happened?"

"I don't know. Jack left me a message when I was in class. I didn't get it until I got out. All he said was Xavier was in an accident and he was on his way to Memorial. I got it about forty minutes after he left it, then spent the last hour trying to find you."

"Is he okay?" I ask as we rush down the stairs.

"I don't know. I don't know if Jack knows. I tried to call him back, but it went to voicemail." She shrugs as we make it outside. "Hopefully we know more when we get there."

I let her lead me to her car. I pull up my phone and type out a quick text to Xavier, asking if he's okay and to please call me. I'm praying he responds, but the longer he goes without answering, the more my heart drops.

If he's not answering, it means he can't answer.

A small part is still hoping he's ignoring me, but I know in my heart that he wouldn't.

By the time we make it to the hospital, my anxiety is through the roof. I barely wait for the car to stop before I'm out the door. Rebecca is hot on my trail, following behind me.

I rush to the desk, barely stopping as I crash into it.

"Excuse me, one of our friends was brought in a while ago because of an accident. Xavier Walsh," Rebecca tells the lady behind the desk calmly.

"Are you family?"

I consider lying, but don't want to be called out.

"No," I rasp.

"I'm sorry, sweetheart. I can't give you any information then."

My heart seizes in my chest. "Please." I feel my eyes prickling with tears. "Please tell me something. I'm begging you."

Her eyes waver. "You're his girlfriend?" she says in a way that tells me she's trying to help me out here. "You should have started with that."

"Sorry, she's a mess. Yes, she's his girlfriend."

"Let me see." She taps away at her keyboard. "Well, I can't tell you anything about his condition, but I can tell you what waiting room to go to. Go up to the second floor. On the right, you will see a waiting room for the surgical unit."

"He's in surgery?" I screech.

The nurse's eyes shift to the security guard as he walks closer. She gives a subtle shake of her head.

"Honey, I suggest you go to the waiting room and when the doctor comes out, you tell them exactly who you are." She gives me a knowing look.

"They can tell you more."

"Come on," Rebecca says under her breath, pulling my arm. "Thank you," she tells the lady.

The lady gives me a sympathetic smile as I'm pulled away.

Rebecca drags me into the elevator as I feel the panic building inside my chest.

No. No. Not again. I can't.

"Breathe," she demands, pushing me to the floor before shoving my head down between my legs.

"Surgery isn't good, Becca," I whimper, tears filling my eyes.

"Stop thinking the worst. He needs all the positive thoughts and prayers he can get," she chastises.

The doors open and she basically drags me out of the elevator and toward the waiting room. She drops my hand, making me look up as she rushes toward Jack. He sits with his arms on his knees, hands covering his face.

"Hey," she whispers, kneeling in front of him.

He drops his hands and weaves them into her hair and buries his face into the crown of her head. I slowly approach and sit down next to them.

"Have you heard anything?" I whisper.

Jack shakes his head, messing up Rebecca's hair. "They won't tell me anything, but Tinsley will be here soon and she will get us some answers."

"Why would Tinsley come?" I bristle.

Jack turns, glaring at me. "This isn't the time for your little jealousy act but if you must know she was on the phone with him when he was hit and she's his emergency contact." He says harshly. "If I were you I would adjust my attitude real fucking quick. This isn't the time and it sure as hell isn't the place."

"You're right." I nod, looking away.

I move a couple seats down to give him his space, while I take a seat, settling in to wait as long as it takes.

"Can I get you anything?" Rebecca asks Jack.

"I just want to hold you." I hear him murmur.

Chill, Cassi, it will all be okay. When Ryan died, we never made it this far.

The music blasting as we drive down the gravel road. I'm sitting in the middle of the back seat, swaying back and forth. Ryan's driving and Jared's in the passenger seat.

"Hey, move over, I want to see if I can hit the sign with the bottle," he says to Ryan.

Ryan moves over as Jared rolls down his window. Once close enough to the road sign, Jared chucks the empty beer bottle out, hitting the pole and not the sign itself.

"Fuck!" he growls, making Ryan and I laugh.

"I thought you were good at throwing things," I tease, pushing on the back of his head.

"Fuck off, Cass," he says, turning and trying to give me a dead leg.

"Hey," I yell, moving my legs just in time.

"Now, now guys. Knock it off. Keep your hands to yourself," Ryan says, amused.

"Yeah, Jared. Keep those hands to yourself. Who knows what you've touched recently that you shouldn't."

"I swear to God, Cass," he hisses.

"Cass, give him another beer and stop teasing him," Ryan says, breaking up yet another fight. "Jared, you know she's just giving you shit."

I had Jared another beer reluctantly. "I made sure not to open it so you know it's not tampered with," I quip.

"How thoughtful."

I lean back and stare out the window.

"Are you sure you don't want a beer?" Jared asks Ryan.

"You know the rules, driver doesn't drink," Ryan chastises.

"Yeah, yeah," Jared says. "So you fucked Becca yet?"

"What the fuck?" Ryan hisses.

"Excuse me?" I demand.

"What she's a hot piece of ass." Jared shrugs.

"What the fuck is wrong with you," Ryan says harshly.

"I'm sorry, but my best friend isn't a whore," I say.

"Trust me, I know. She's a stuck-up fucking prude like you," he spews.

I reach forward and punch the back of his shoulder.

"Fuck you!"

"No fuck you, Cassi!" he hisses, turning in his seat trying to get at me.

"Guys knock it off!" Ryan demands, trying to grab on to Jared's shirt and pull him back into his seat. "Oh, fuck!"

I feel Ryan slam on the breaks and the back end of the car fishtail.

"Ryan," I yell, scared.

"Get control, man," Jarred hisses.

"I'm trying," Ryan says with fear in his voice.

Then I feel it and close my eyes tight. We roll once, twice, and a third time. I whip from one side of the back seat to the other like a rag doll until we come to a stop on the driver's side. I can't help but whimper as I take stock of myself and "Roll On" by Kid Rock plays.

Nothing feels broken.

"Cass." Jared looks back at me. "You okay?"

"I think so. You?"

"Yeah, I'm going to open the door and get you out. You'll have to jump down," he tells me.

"Okay," I whisper, trying to push off my side.

Jared struggles to get the door open but after a couple of tries gets it to stay.

"Climb up. Use the side of the seat as a step to boost you. I'll lift you."

I do as he says and with no time he has me sitting on the edge of the car on the frame.

"Jump out and down."

I do as he says and whimper when I land. My ankle throbbing.

"You okay?" he asks frantically.

"I'm okay, just get down here."

With less grace and more struggle, Jared finally jumps down. I hobble into his arms and embrace him.

"I'm going to call 9-1-1, okay?" he whispers. "Stay where I can see you."

I nod against his chest and pull away. Jared gets on the phone and starts relaying our location.

Ryan.

"Ryan," I whisper, frantically looking around.

"Cass." Jared tries to grab me, but I move around him and around the car.

There. Laying halfway out the window, crushed under the car, is my brother.

"Ryan!" I screech. Running over, I fall to my knees. Hands shaking, not knowing where to touch him. "Ryan," I whisper as tears fall down my face. I brush his hair off his forehead as I look at his pale skin and blue lips.

"Cass," Jared says, full of anguish. He comes up behind me and pulls me into him.

"No! I need to touch him," I say, sobbing.

I latch on to my cold brother's hand and break down.

"It's all my fault, I'm sorry, Cass. It's all my fault," Jared chants in the background.

I don't know how long after I hear the sirens and I hold on tighter.

"Miss, you need to let go," someone whispers, touching my shoulder.

I look over my shoulder, "I can't. He's my brother, I can't leave him. He wouldn't leave me."

"Cassi," someone says, pulling me out of my thoughts. I blink and see Rebecca, frowning. "You okay?"

"Yeah, sure."

"You're shaking."

"I am?" I ask, voice shaking. I clear my throat. "Where's Jack?"

"Tinsley and her family got here. Her brother got us moved into a private waiting room. We should get in there," she says as she rubs my shoulder. "Are you sure you're okay?"

"I am." I stand on wobbly legs.

"I would understand if this brought up some terrible memories," she prods.

"I'm fine. Promise. Let's get in there. I want to know if they know anything."

"Okay, but I'm here." She takes my hand and pulls me into another room. "I know I was a little short with you on the way here, but I needed to get here. I'm sorry."

"It's okay. We're all a little on edge."

"You know Jack didn't mean it either. He adores you."

My heart pangs. I know Jack didn't mean it, but it was painful to hear.

"I know," I say, motioning for her to show me the way.

She leads me down the hall to a new area. Then she opens the door.

Stepping inside, I see there are more people. A lot more people. Two guys and two females.

Tinsley.

I see her standing, wrapped in an attractive man's arms as a blonde woman rubs her arm. The man holding hands with the blonde looks like he could be related to Tinsley.

I know I should go say something, but I'm at a loss for words. I don't think Tinsley ever likes me much, but I know she has to hate me by now.

Instead of going to her, I make my way over to Jack.

Taking a seat next to him, I ask, "Have you heard anything?"

Jack goes to speak, but another voice beats him to it.

"He has a broken arm in two places. They did surgery to put it in a bunch of metal so he can heal," the man holding Tinsley says gruffly. "You must be Cassi."

"Be nice," Tinsley chastises him. "How are you holding up?" She turns to ask me.

"I'm okay, you?"

"I've been better." She sighs.

"I never want to hear you scream like that again," her man says.

"Agreed," the dark-haired man says.

"I'm Sage," the beautiful blonde says with an open smile, walking over to me to shake my hand. "This is my boyfriend Reed, Tinsley's brother." She smiles up at her man, who looks at her like she hung the moon. "And Casanova over there is Finley, Tinsley's boyfriend. We've heard a lot about you."

"I would say nice to meet you, but." I smile awkwardly.

"That would be a lie." Sage smirks.

"Are his parents coming?" I ask no one in particular.

"One would think if you were so close to Xavier, you would know he's basically estranged from his parents. That's what happens when you fight their demands and go against what they want," Reed's unkind voice says, leaning against the wall before pulling Sage into him, away from me.

"They are both over in Europe currently. They told me to keep them updated," Tinsley says softly while nibbling on her lip.

"Hey, stop that," Finley scolds her, pulling her lip free. "That's my lip to torture." He smirks, making her blush.

"Could you not?" Reed demands, making the girls laugh.

The entire room sobers as soon as the door opens.

The doctor walks in. "Is this the family of Xavier Walsh?"

"We are," Reed tells him.

Tinsley steps forward. "I'm Xavier's power of attorney. How is he?"

"Would you like to go somewhere private?" the doctor asks her, looking at our large group.

"Anything you have to say, you can say in front of us," Sage tells him.

The doctor doesn't take her word, instead looking to Tinsley.

"They are his family. Anything you tell me, I'll turn around and tell them, anyway."

"Very well."

The doctor goes into detail about how they reset Xavier's arm. How many pins and bolts he needed. How he lost consciousness for a few moments, but came to before he made it to the hospital. That he has a concussion and how they had to glue shut a cut on his forehead.

The entire time the doctor is talking, my heart is racing. The pain that started earlier being amplified by hearing how hurt he is.

"Overall, he was lucky," the doctor finishes.

"When can we see him?" Tinsley asks, heartache in her voice.

"Once they have him moved into a private room, someone will come get you. Only two of you at a time to start off with. We don't want to overwhelm the patient."

"Thank you, doctor," Reed says. The rest of us murmur our thanks as well.

Tinsley moves away from their group on the far side of the room, coming to where I'm standing in the corner.

"You don't have to be way back here. I know my brother and boyfriend can be intimidating, but it's not you. They have a hard time trusting."

My eyes tear up at her words. "Why are you being so nice to me right now?"

Her eyes show understanding.

"Let's take a walk. I think we should talk."

"Where are you going, woman?" Finley calls from across the room.

"For a walk. I'll be back. Call me if they come back."

He doesn't look happy, but he doesn't say anything else.

Leading me out of the waiting room, she leads me down the hall in silence. She doesn't stop until we are at the elevators. She leads me to the love seat positioned across from the elevators.

Once settled, she lets out a heavy sigh.

"I know why you think I wouldn't like you. Xavier told me everything, but I think you have the wrong idea. You know there are three sides to every story. There's your side. There's Xavier's. Then there's the truth. I think you both have vilified yourself in your own versions. He has never said one negative thing about you."

"He should. I broke up with him."

She gives me a sad smile. "Yes, you did. His heart is aching, but you made valid points. If I'm not mistaken, I feel like you might have broken your own heart in the process as well."

I give her a small smile, showing her she's on the right track.

"I saw it when I came down before. Xavier cares deeply for you. I saw your face when he called you a friend. After you ran off, I read him the riot act. I couldn't believe he would treat you so carelessly. Do you know what he told me?" When I shake my head no, she continues, "He said that you had some emotional scars you were working through and that he didn't want to scare you off by using more serious labels."

"He's the one who took dating off the table. I would have dated him from the start," I tell her.

"I know. He told me that too. He wouldn't tell me why, but I knew why. I'm assuming Xavier told you our past?"

"He did."

"Good. He needed to. I'm always going to be his friend, but the past couple months? I'm no longer his best friend. That's you. You're who he is confiding in. Who he spends all of his time with. He cares about you."

"I care about him too. When Rebecca told me he was in the hospital, I flipped out. I'm still anxious even though the doctor told us he would be okay. Like I won't believe it until I see him for myself."

She gives me a warm smile, reaching out to grab my hand. "He's lucky to have you."

I let out a sigh. "No offense, but your boyfriend made it seem like I wasn't even welcome here."

She laughs. "Like Finley would know anything about Xavier would want. They aren't exactly the best of friends. He doesn't know Xavier like you or I do. He doesn't know that you didn't ask about his parents because you don't know about their relationship, but because you know it would mean the world to him if they showed up. Just like you know it's going to hurt like hell when he finds out they didn't bother to come. Trust me, Xavier would want you here."

"Thank you," I murmur.

"You're welcome. I think that if we talked more, we could be friends. Besides, I need someone to team up on Xavier with."

She bumps my knee with hers as she giggles.

I give her a warm smile. "I'm sorry if I was cold to you before."

She gives me a knowing smile in return. "If some chick showed up hugging on my man, I would be a little more than upset, even if he told me they were just friends. No worries."

"Tin tin, they are ready to let us back."

We turn and see Finley call from down the hall.

"Coming," she calls to him.

She pulls me up, wrapping her arm in mine. Once we get back to the waiting room, she announces, "Cassi and I are going to go back first."

No one questions her.

The nurse leads us down some halls and through a set of automatic doors. Once at the room, she stops. "He's still out, but he should come to shortly. They already started weaning him off the medicine to help him recover."

We both nod before she turns to walk away.

Tinsley steps forward, pushing the door open before taking a step in. She holds the door, turning to look back at me.

I can't meet her eyes though. All I can see is Xavier lying on the bed.

"Avi," I breathe out, my eyes prickling with tears.

He is lying in the bed, eyes closed, looking so peaceful.

Just like Ryan did.

My heart beats frantically as I try to reconcile what I'm seeing in front of me and the memories in my head.

He looks like he's at peace. Like he is sleeping in on a Saturday morning.

Looks deceive. He's no longer here with us. I hear my mom sob next to me. My heart breaks for her and for my father who is standing next to her, cradling her in his arms, attempting to keep it together. He has his own tears streaming down.

I take a couple steps forward toward the bed. Once at the side, I reach out, brushing his hand.

It's cold to the touch. Not warm like it usually is. His chest isn't moving. His eyes aren't fluttering behind the eyelids. His skin is pale, a bluish tint setting in.

My heart cracks, looking at my best friend. My brother. The tears fall easily as my head pounds with the pressure. I cling to that cold hand, willing my life force into his.

I can't live without him. How am I going to live without him?

This is all my fault. I shouldn't be here, he should be. He was the responsible one. The good child.

I pull his hand up to my lips, pressing a quick kiss to it before turning and running from the room.

No one calls after me. No one runs after me.

I'm all alone.

I lost him.

Ryan.

That same cracking feeling hits my chest, warning me I'm about to crumble.

"Cassi?" Tinsley's voice drifts to me, but I can't answer her.

Instead, I shake my head at her, backing away from the door. Her eyes hold concern, but I can't. I can't go in there.

"I can't do this. I'm sorry," I sob.

Then I'm running.

This isn't the same hospital. This isn't even the same city, but the feeling is the same.

The helplessness. The desperation. The complete and utter desolation of my heart.

I don't stop running until I'm in the stairwell, bent over attempting to breathe through my tears.

I hear the door open behind me, but I can't acknowledge anyone.

"Come here."

Before I know it, I'm in Jack's arms as I sob into his chest. I stand there, letting the raw emotions pour from my body until I'm weak.

"Let's get you home," Jack murmurs.

I let him lead me out of the hospital, away from the memories.

Away from Xavier.

Xavier

My phone rings as I slide into my car.

"Hey, give me a sec to connect the Bluetooth."

"Sure."

I start my car and wait for the Bluetooth to connect. "Alright. What's up?" I ask as I slide my phone into the holder on the dash, making sure the camera can see me.

"Just checking in," Tinsley says, making me sigh.

"I'm fine," I say as I pull out of the parking lot.

"Yeah, but your single." She pouts.

"Isn't the first time, won't be the last," I tease as I drive. "Now tell me something good."

Tinsley fills me in on what's new with her and her family.

"Sage bought home a puppy the other day and let's just say that Reed isn't too thrilled."

"Oh? Why not?" I smirk as I pull up to the stoplight.

Tinsley giggles, making me smile. "The dog may or may not have an obsession with eating all of Reed's left shoes. Doesn't matter if it's a dress shoe or one of his chucks, it's always a left one."

"So he only has right shoes?" I laugh.

"Yep. It doesn't even matter if he puts them up. Somehow the little sucker gets them. Sage thinks it's hilarious."

The light turns green and I go. "Because it is."

Right as I pull into the intersection, I see a flash out of the corner of my eye. I turn my head and see it right before it happens. First, I feel the impact, then another, mixed with the screeching of metal and Tinsley's screams.

"Oh, fuck! Reed, get the plane!" a male voice says over the speaker right as everything goes black.

⚜

I GROAN, TRYING to turn over, but find something stopping me.

"Hey, it's okay. Don't move too much."

My eyes flutter open. "What?" I attempt to say, but my throat is dry.

"Hold on. The nurse said I could give you some water if you woke up."

My eyes take in the room, coming to land on the face for the voice. After she brings the straw to my mouth and I'm able to wet my throat, I speak again.

"What are you doing here, Tins? What happened?"

Her eyes are sad. "We were on the phone when you got into a car accident. We got on the first plane here."

"We?"

She laughs. "Finley, Sage, and Reed."

I go to laugh, but wince at the pain.

Fuck, my head hurts.

"How bad am I hurt?"

"You fractured your arm. I'm afraid you'll set off metal detectors for the rest of your life. Other than that, just some scrapes and bruises."

"No wonder I feel like I got hit by a truck."

Her eyes widen at my phrase, but I chuckle then wince again.

"Don't joke like that. I thought we were going to lose you."

"Nah, you can't get rid of my man that easily," an unfamiliar voice says from the door.

I smile when I see Jack, holding the biggest teddy bear in his arms, comes waltzing in the door.

"Here you go, boo. The lady downstairs in the gift shop assured me this is the best gift to show you want the person you care about to get better."

"Don't make me laugh, asshole. It hurts."

He smiles widely at me. "Oh come on. You complaining about a fractured arm? You pussy."

I know he's joking, using his humor to hide his concern. I can see it on his face. He was worried.

"I know, right? Looks like no video games for me for a while."

He laughs. "That's okay. I'll just play with Ace."

My heart twinges in pain.

Cassi.

"Who's Ace?" Tinsley asks.

Jack's face sobers. "Cassi."

"Oh." Tinsley turns to me. "She was here, you know."

My heart stutters. "What?"

"Yeah. She was here, but when she got to the room, she took off."

My heart aches for her. I bet she hasn't even been to a hospital since Ryan. My body aches to reach out to her.

Ignoring Tinsley, I turn to Jack. "Is she okay? You should be with her right now."

He gives me a sad look. "She's okay. She was a little shook seeing you like this, but I took her home. Rebecca stayed with her. She said she'd keep me updated."

"I'm fine. I need you to go watch over her. She needs someone."

He walks over to the bed. "She has someone. She has Rebecca. Rebecca said she was planning to head home for the break on Friday, anyway. I'll go check on her until then, but then she'll be with her parents."

"Go take her dinner. Please, man. I know you're concerned, but Tinsley is here with me. She needs you more."

He sighs. "You really love her, don't you?"

Swallowing hard, I nod, not caring about the pain.

"Fuck. Fine. I'll go check on her, but when you're discharged, I'm taking your ass home. No question."

"Deal."

I watch as he heads back out, bringing my attention back to Tinsley.

"Is she going to be okay? I didn't understand why she left, but you make it sound like it's a big deal."

I sigh. "It's not my story to tell, Tin. Hospitals hold bad memories for her. I'm surprised she was even able to walk in. It's killing me I can't be with her right now. If she'd even want me with her."

She gives me a sad smile. "I think she wants you more than you realize. I think she's battling her own demons right now, though. Give her time. She'll come back around."

"I'll give her all the time she needs." Changing the subject, I clear my throat. "So what does it take to get some more water?"

She shakes her head, laughing. "Why are men such babies when they get sick or hurt? Finley acts like he's dying when he gets a cold."

"Hey, I got hit by a truck."

She sighs. "Yeah. Yeah. That was so five minutes ago."

I shake my head. "To think, I made you my power of attorney."

She laughs. "Hey, you're the one who trusted me."

"I know. Thank you for coming Tinsley."

She smiles at me. "Anytime. Your family."

CHAPTER EIGHTEEN

Cassi

The past couple of days have been a mess. Even though Jack assured me Xavier is fine, that block on my chest is still there. Add in the whirling emotions leftover from the hospital and I'm not sure where my head's at anymore. Part of me wanted to see him, but I didn't want to upset him in his condition. I know he would see it was a step in getting back together, when I'm not sure I'm ready for that yet.

I know Xavier came home yesterday, and I knew it was only a matter of time before he came to see me. Jack told me he was recovering well and even received clearance to drive.

"I'm so happy to have you home." Mama squeezes me for the umpteenth time.

"It's only for a couple of weeks. I do still have school. Besides, I come home on the weekends all the time."

She smiles. "I know, but I still miss you when you're away. Jerry, look at our baby all grown up. Coming back from her first semester at college."

"Stop smothering the girl or else she won't come back next time," Dad teases.

"As if you could keep me away." I walk over and hug him.

"This will always be your home, baby girl. Even when you have your own children running around," he reminds me.

"Then I'll be dropping them rascals off with you every time they cause me trouble," I warn.

"Then we will ply them with sugar for hours and send them home just like Mama always did to us." Mama comes around to wrap her arm around Dad.

"Evil. Pure evil," I glare.

"Karma. Pure Karma." Mama winks.

"Whatever. I thought we were going to bake some cookies."

She smiles brightly at me. "Of course we are. Let's get to baking."

"That's my cue to get out of here." Dad pats my shoulder, heading out of the kitchen, toward the living room.

"He doesn't know it, but I bought him a new TV for Christmas. It's an eighty-inch, much bigger than the sixty. You think he'll like it?" Mom whispers.

I giggle. "I think he'll love it."

"Good."

We work in silence for a little bit, each knowing our task at hand. I've been making cookies with my mom for years. I don't think I even need to look at the recipe card anymore, even though it's sitting on the counter next to me. Ryan used to sit with Dad sometimes, but other times, he would sit at the counter, taste testing each batch. He'd always say, "I'm testing to make sure it's not poisoned."

We knew he was full of it, but Mom let him do it.

"Honey, are you okay?"

I startle at Mom's words. "What?"

That's when I feel it. The tears falling down my face.

"You're crying. What's wrong?"

I shake my head. "I was thinking about Ryan."

She wipes her hand on her apron, moving to pull me in for a hug. "I miss him too."

"I think we all do. Jared's going to counseling, you know."

She gives me a sad smile. "Laura told me. It seems to be helping him a lot."

"I think I want to try it."

She nods. "Then that's what we will do. There's no shame in going to therapy. Your father and I went for a couple months after Ryan."

"What? Why didn't you tell me?"

"We tried talking about it with you once, but you shut down. We decided it was best to wait until you were ready."

"Thank you. I'm so sorry I was so selfish all of them months."

"Don't be. I think we all were a bit selfish, working through our own stuff. No need to apologize for it now."

"Thanks, Mama."

We get back to baking, laughing, and joking the entire time. Then once we're done, we start on dinner. It's the best day I've had in a while.

That's why a knock at the door catches me off guard.

"I got it," Daddy calls from the hall.

I hear the murmur of voices. Curious, I move closer, straining to hear.

"Hey, Jerry. Happy Holidays."

Xavier. I would recognize his voice anywhere.

"Happy Holidays. What did you do to your arm, son?"

"Car accident. I'm okay though. I just wanted to drop this off for Cass. Can you make sure she gets it?"

"You can give it to her yourself. Cass, the doors for you."

Rounding the corner, my heart catches in my chest.

I haven't seen Xavier since the day at the hospital when he was hooked up to all the tubes and wires.

He looks much better now. His arm is in a cast as he holds it out to the side awkwardly. He has a box in his other arm, but other than that he looks good.

Then his eyes meet mine and I'm frozen.

Then he glances away, releasing me.

I let out the deep breath I was holding, revealing myself to them.

"What are you doing here?" I step closer to the door.

"Cass," he breathes out. "How are you?"

I look behind me to see my dad still watching. I grab my jacket from the hook, ushering him outside.

"I'll be right back, Dad."

"Yeah, no problem. Maybe Xavier wants to stay for dinner?" Dad asks.

"Maybe. I'll ask." I shut the door behind me.

Xavier steps forward. "I won't stay for dinner unless you want me to."

I move past him, leading him closer to the car he must have rented since his was totaled.

"What are you here for? You shouldn't be driving."

He gives me a small smile. "I was cleared for driving. I just wanted to give you, your Christmas gift."

"I don't need anything."

"I know, but I wanted to get you something."

"I didn't get you anything."

"I don't need anything."

"Do you have an answer for everything?"

He laughs. "No."

"Well, I don't feel right accepting it from you."

His eyes fall. "It was made especially for you. I can't take it back."

I let out a deep sigh. "Okay."

I reach out, grabbing the box. His finger brushes against mine, making my heart stutter.

"I know you were mad at me before," he starts, his finger lingering on mine. "I wanted to apologize. I know I made a mistake, and it was wrong. I don't deserve your forgiveness for the way I acted, but I hope you find comfort in my words. I hope you have a Merry Christmas."

My walls crack as he walks past me to his driver's door. I remember what he said on Thanksgiving.

What if he doesn't have anywhere to go?

"Wait." I spin, unable to keep myself from asking, "What are you doing for Christmas Break?"

He turns, giving me a sad smile. "If I said nothing, would you invite me to stay with you?"

I bite my lip, considering his words.

Would I?

He lets out a laugh. "I'm joking. Don't worry about me, Adra. I can take care of myself."

I take a couple steps forward, setting the gift on his hood before grabbing his uninjured arm.

"Seriously, Avi, where are you going for break?" I look up into his eyes.

For half a second, I worry that he's going to tell me he's going to spend it with Tinsley. Why it would matter, I don't know. I know they are just friends. I'm not even jealous of her anymore. Or at least I shouldn't be.

Didn't I end this? Aren't I the one keeping us apart?

One word could keep him here.

Stay.

That's all it would take for him to wrap me into his arms and accept me back.

One word caught in my throat because of fear. Fear that I can't trust his feelings. Fuck, I can't trust my own feelings right now.

"I'm going home with Jack. I hear his mama makes a mean brisket for the holidays. I can't wait to figure out what that means." He steps closer to me, pulling me into a brief hug, before backing up to pull my face to his.

It's just a ghost of a kiss across my lips, but the heat it spreads throughout my body is an inferno. The memories it elicits causes me to shiver.

"Sorry. I had to have one last taste of heaven. I'll be fine. I don't want you worrying about me. It's cold out. You should get inside to your family.

Have an amazing holiday. Maybe when classes start back up, I'll see you on campus."

He opens his door then, getting inside the car. When the door closes, it jerks me from my frozen place.

I grab my gift, making my way back to the door. I turn to look before going in and smile. He waves at me once before motioning for me to go inside.

Ever the gentleman.

Once inside, I peek out the side window and watch him leave.

"He didn't want to stay for dinner?" Dad asks from behind me.

"He did, but he's spending the holidays with his friend Jack. He didn't want to make him wait too long."

"Ah. He's a good one. Always considerate. He's taken quite a liking to you, pumpkin. What is it he got for you?"

I hustle toward the stairs. "It's private, Daddy. I'm not going to open it until Christmas. I'm going to put it in my room."

"Okay, but hurry back. Mama says dinner's done."

I rush up to my room, placing the gift on the dresser. Part of me is curious what he might have bought me. What does Xavier think I want for Christmas? I could find out now, but that's not me. I'm not the one who opens gifts early and begs to know what I got. I love the spirit of Christmas. I love giving gifts more than receiving, but even then, I like being surprised by what someone might think I want.

Smiling, I rub my hand across the perfectly wrapped present. I can't wait to find out what he thought I would want.

Xavier

"You sure you are good? I can take you to the airport," Jack says as he zips up his last bag.

"Yep. My flight's not for a while. I'll get a cab there or something."

"Alright, man. If you change your mind or come home early, call me. Ma would love to have you."

"I know. If Tinsley lets me come home early, I'll call you."

"Alright. See you after winter break. Have a great holiday."

"You too."

As soon as the door shuts, I let my smile fall. It's exhausting faking a smile all the time.

After my trip out to Cassi's house, I tried to play it off like it didn't hurt me as badly as it did.

Truth is, seeing her, but not being with her hurt me worse than the truck that hit me did. My chest has felt tight ever since.

Jack could tell I'd been off, but thankfully he let me alone.

He invited me home with him for Christmas, but I couldn't stomach the thought of being social.

It's the same reason I told Tinsley I was going home with Jack when she asked me to come home. She misses me, but I can't imagine being around her right now.

Not because I still have feelings for her, but because my misplaced feelings for her are part of the reason, I lost Cassi. It's not her fault, but I can't bear being around her and Finley.

Rubbing my hand down my face, I shake off my thoughts.

Pulling out my laptop, I put a movie on.

Hours later, a knock at the door wakes me.

Answering the door, I find a short, pudgy man on the other side.

"You're supposed to be gone. You can't stay here."

"It's my dorm. Why can't I stay?"

"School rules. Students have to vacate during break. It's my job to make sure everyone's left."

"Come on, man. I have nowhere to go."

He shrugs. "Nothing I can do."

Sighing, I pull out my wallet. "Would a couple hundred dollars change your mind?"

He looks down at the five hundred-dollar bills. "It might make me turn a blind eye, but if anyone catches you, I know nothing."

"Deal." I hand him the cash.

"Merry Christmas."

"You too," I grumble as he makes his way to the next door.

Then I head back to my bed, determined to sleep the entire break.

CHAPTER NINETEEN

Cassi

"**D**idn't Xavier bring you a gift?" Dad asks as he's cleaning up the living room.

We had a pretty tame Christmas compared to years past, but there were still plenty of presents. It was bittersweet. I could tell we were all missing Ryan, but we muscled through, creating new memories. It wasn't perfect, but it would do for now.

"He did. I think I'll open that one in my room though."

Mom laughs. "Why don't you go do that, honey? I'll start with dinner."

"Okay. Thanks."

I give them each a hug, running up to my room.

I won't lie. I wanted to open his gift first thing this morning, but I must be a masochist. I made myself stop. I made myself wait, knowing it would be hard to resist the urge to text him once I saw whatever gift he got me.

Sitting on the edge of my bed, I hold the box in my lap. I start by carefully unwrapping the paper. A plain brown box greets me. Pulling the tape from the top, I slowly open the flaps.

Then I gaze inside.

My eyes burn with unshed tears as I take in the object.

I pull it out, no longer able to hold it in.

He's perfect.

That's all I can think as I stare at the piece of wood in my hands.

No, the tree.

That's what it is. Xavier somehow was able to get the part of the tree that I showed him, which held mine and Ryan's initials. Not only was he able to remove it without damaging it, he made it into something I could hang on the wall. The reminder of that memory that means so much to me.

The box falls to the floor as I hold it to my chest, hugging it as if I was hugging Ryan. I let the mixture of grief and relief fill my body.

I miss Ryan so much. This gift means more to me than anything anyone else could have gotten me. The only thing that could best it would be bringing Ryan back, which is impossible.

I rock back and forth until I'm able to calm down. As soon as I have a grip on my emotions, I move to grab my phone, but a card on the floor captures my attention.

I pick it up, seeing the nickname Xavier calls me across the front of the envelope.

Adra.

My heart hammers, not sure I'm ready to read his words, but knowing I have to. I cannot stop myself.

Adra,

I'm not sure if I'm doing the right thing anymore, but I hope I am. I know how much this meant to you and Ryan. I know you were worried it would disappear one day. I wanted to take that anxiety away from you. I would do anything to keep you from feeling the pain of that loss again. I hope you look at this every day and remember that even if Ryan isn't here with you physically, he will always be in your heart.

Love,

Avi

In that moment, I knew what I had to do.

I pick up the phone, dialing Xavier's number.

When it goes straight to voicemail, I curse. Then I dial Jack.

"What's up, Ace? Miss me yet?"

"Never, but I'm sure Rebecca might," I tease.

"Wait. Does she really?"

I shake my head at his antics. "A best friend never tells. Anyway, I need to talk to Xavier, but his phone is off. Can you get him for me?"

"I would love to, but he's not with me. He's at Tinsley's."

My heart stops. Did he lie to me because he didn't want to hurt me?

"He told me he was spending Christmas with you." I frown. "Never mind, I don't have her number. Fuck."

"I have her number. Hold on. I'll call you right back."

I pace in my room, feeling an undeniable need to be with Xavier. I really want to see him, but talking to him will have to do until he comes back.

When my phone rings, I half expect it to be Xavier, ready to tell him how I feel, but it's Jack.

"Jack?"

"He's not there either. She said he told her he was staying with me too. I have no idea where he is. I'm getting in the truck now."

"Shit. How far are you?"

"A couple hours at least."

"Don't head this way yet. I'm only thirty minutes from campus. I'll go look around and see if I can figure out where he would go. At Thanksgiving, he was planning to stay in a hotel. I bet he did that."

"Okay. You go look and I'll call hotels."

"Call me if you find anything."

"You too."

Xavier

POUNDING ON MY door startles me awake. I stumble to the door, careful of my cast.

Fucking thing keeps getting in my way.

I open the door, expecting campus security, but find an angel on the other side.

"Adra, what are you doing here?"

"Me? What are you doing here? You said you were with Jack. You lied." She smacks my chest.

"Ow. Still injured," I say in jest. "Merry Christmas to you too."

"Whatever. Were you sleeping? It's noon."

I shrug. "Didn't sleep well. I didn't have any big plans today."

"Why didn't you tell me you had nowhere to go? My parents would have let you stay."

"It's not that I had nowhere to go. Jack would've let me go home with him. Tinsley begged me to come home to her. I didn't feel like being around people."

"Why? You shouldn't be alone on Christmas."

I let out a humorless laugh. "I've been alone more Christmases than I can count. I'm okay. Really, Adra. You can go home and spend the day with your family."

She sighs. "Avi."

"It's okay. I heard you loud and clear. I fucked up. I was up in my head and I messed it up. Jack warned me it had to be the right time for it to work with one of them girls. With the only girl."

"I'm going to pretend I know what being one of them girls means and ignore the rest of that nonsense. I thought about what you said. It wasn't all you. It was me too. I was caught up in my head too and let it affect us. I talked to my parents. It had nothing to do with you and everything to do with me. Everything to do with the fact that I haven't dealt with the death of Ryan. Your gift brought that clarity. That was the sweetest, most selfless thing you could have given me," she chokes up.

"Baby, don't cry. Please. I can't take any more of your tears. I'm supposed to make you happy, not sad."

"These aren't tears of sadness. They are tears of gratitude. Opening that gift to find that piece of wood polished and looking nice. Being able to trace our initials? That did something for me. It helped me see that I've been avoiding processing my grief for Ryan. I haven't given myself a chance to heal. I want to heal now. I'm going to start going to counseling for a while. I want to be a healthier me. I had already had it figured out with my mom before you even came over."

"I'm happy to hear that, Adra. I want you to heal too. I want you to be happy."

"You want to know the funny thing about that?"

"What?"

"When Ryan died, I didn't think I would ever be happy again. I did some things to try to feel something. Anything other than the agonizing grief I was feeling. I was surviving, but I wasn't living. Then I met you. You changed that for me. I was happy with you. No. I am happy with you. Avi, I know what I said the other day, but after some time to reflect, I don't want this to end. I don't want us to end."

My heart races. "What are you saying?"

"I'm yours, Avi. That is, if you'll still have me."

I pull her into my arms and kiss her hard. "I've always been yours. Even when we didn't know each other, I was yours." Kiss. "Fuck. I didn't think I would ever get to kiss you again."

She giggles. "You missed kissing me?"

"Fuck yeah. Holding you. Kissing you. Talking to you. Waking up next to you. I missed it all. That's why I didn't want to see anyone today. I wanted to miss you in peace."

"Well now, that you don't have to miss me, come home with me. Mom pretty much demanded it when I told her I thought you were spending Christmas alone."

"Well, I can't disappoint my future mother-in-law."

"You're so silly. Jumping ahead of yourself, aren't you?"

"Not at all. When you meet one of them girls, you marry her. One day, Cassandra May Davis, I will marry you."

EPILOGUE

Cassi

FOUR YEARS LATER
Graduation Day

I sit in the stands with Tinsley and Finley on my left and my parents on my right. My graduation already over.

"I'm so excited," Tinsley gushes for the thousandth time since we sat down.

"Trust me, we know you are, Tin," Finley says as he squeezes her knee.

I smile as the two of them fall into each other.

They are something else.

"They are something else," my mother says under her breath with a smile on her face.

"You get used to it."

When I met them we didn't get off on the best start, but over the years, we've found our way.

I sit back and think about all the things that have happened since Avi came into my life. Going into sophomore year, Jack and Avi decided they didn't want to be in the dorms, so they bought a house together. By junior year I moved in and going into senior year Rebecca did as well. Late-night arguments about who knows what. Study dates and holidays. We've done it all together.

It's a little sad thinking of the four of us no longer being together on a daily basis. Avi and I have had our ups and downs as a couple, same with Jack and Rebecca, but that's their story to tell. Or not. But in the end, we made it out together.

"What time is your flight?" Finley asks, pulling me out of my head.

"Nine tonight."

"Still no idea where you're going?" He smirks.

"Not a clue." I sigh. "Any chance you'll tell me?"

"Not a chance in hell." He laughs.

"I guess I will find out in a few hours," I muse. "Xavier does love surprising me."

Xavier

My eyes shift between a sleeping Cassi and the view outside the window. The sun rising behind the Eiffel Tower. I roll the ring between my fingers and smile.

She doesn't know.

For the last year, I've been carrying this ring around with me, waiting for the perfect time to put it on her finger. Taking pictures of me holding it with her in the background, completely clueless. As Cassi lays sleeping, I slip it onto her left hand and just stare at it.

What if I left it there? Toss my original plan out the window and do something simple, like this.

Cassi shifts in her sleep, tucking her left hand under her chin.

Shit. The ring.

For a moment, I panic. I can't reach the ring.

Fuck it.

"Adra." I shake her.

Cass hums.

"Time to wake up, beautiful," I tell her as I brush some hair away from her face.

"Unless there is coffee and those French pastries you promised me, I'm not moving," she rasps, making me laugh.

"Don't worry, room service should bring them up any minute."

I hold my breath as Cassi brings her left hand up to her mouth, yawning.

She freezes with her fist to her mouth, the ring staring back at her.

"Avi," she says breathlessly.

"I told you I was going to marry you one day," I say nervously. "Marry me, Cassandra May. Be my wife. Build a life with me."

Her eyes fill with tears. "Of course I'll marry you." She laughs.

I lean down as she sits up, meeting in the middle as we kiss.

"I love you," we say in unison.

Our kiss turns heated as I climb under the covers, pulling her body into mine.

"How about we spend the day in bed?" Cassi whispers in my ear.

"I think that can be arranged," I tell her as I toss the blanket over our heads, blocking out the world.

I may have spent my life rich with money, but now with Cassi by my side, I'm far richer than I could have ever imagined.

The End.

Thank you for reading One of Them Girls. We hope you loved this story as much as we do. Looking for more from us? Check out our Trailer Park Girls Duet, starting with Mayhem available now on Amazon and Kindle Unlimited.

Want to stay up to date on our newest releases and access to exclusive content? Sign up for our newsletter now!

Author Bio:

Cala Riley, better known as Cala and Riley, are a pair of friends with a deep-seated love of books and writing. Both Cala and Riley are happily married and each have children, Cala with the four-legged kind while Riley has a mixture of both two-legged and four. While they live apart, that does not affect their connection. They are the true definition of family. What started as an idea that quickly turned into a full-length book and a bond that will never end.

Acknowledgements

Husbands/Family- Thank you for loving us through the crazy and listening to us ramble.

Ashley Estep- Thank you for staying on us to make sure we stayed on schedule.

Louise O'Reilly- Thank you for being you.

Jenny Dicks- Thank you for all the swoons & ideas.

Aimee Henry- Thank you for loving the stories as much as we do.

Nikki Pennington- For listening to our rambles and talking us off of ledges.

My Brothers Editor/ Elle- Thank you for being the most laid back editor and making the entire process painless.

Books and Moods- Thank you for everything that you do for us. From covers to formatting and just being a cheerleader in our corner.

Bloggers/Readers- Thank you for loving our stories as much as we do and spreading the word.

Also by Author

Brighton Academy Series

Unbidden

Unpredictable

Undeniably

Unapologetically

Mafia Royalty Series

Mafia King

Mafia Underboss

Mafia Prince

The Syndicates Series

Matteo

Killian

Haruaki

Nikolai

Enzo

Callum

Trailer Park Girls Duet

Mayhem

Harmony

Shadow Crew Series
Redlined

Friction

Shift

Finish Line

Standalone
One of Them Girls

Where to Find Us

Facebook

Instagram

TikTok

Bookbub

Goodreads

Amazon

Cala Riley's Boudoir of Sin

Website

Newsletter

Printed in Dunstable, United Kingdom